"That kiss meant something."

His eyelids dropped a fraction over his very warm gaze, seductive and intent. Making her feel restless and needy. She half wished he'd kiss her again.

She posed the question that had plagued her ever since. "Why *did* you kiss me back then, Clay?"

"Because that mouth... I thought... We both—" He broke off and blew out a loud breath. "To hell with the past, Sarah."

With a dangerous glint in his eyes, he started toward her. Unable to move, she swallowed. "What are you doing?"

"What I've wanted to do since you knocked on my door this morning." He cupped her face between his big rough hands and brushed her bangs back with his fingers.

"Please, Clay," she whispered, not sure whether she wanted him to let go of her or step closer.

The corner of his mouth rose. Angling his head, he leaned toward her....

Dear Reader,

This is the fourth book of my miniseries set in Saddlers Prairie, a fictitious ranching town in Montana prairie country.

Have you ever wondered what happens to a rodeo star when his career ends? I have, and I decided to explore the issue. Clay Hollyer is a former bull-riding champion whose career ended after a nasty run-in with a bull. He now has a new life in Saddlers Prairie.

Sarah Tigarden is searching for her biological mother, who once lived in Saddlers Prairie. She and Clay met three years ago, when she interviewed him for a magazine article.

I don't want to spoil the story, so I'll just say that they didn't exactly part on good terms. Not an auspicious beginning for the hero and heroine of a romance novel, you may be thinking.

Which makes this story all the more interesting.

Happy reading!

Ann

P.S. I always appreciate hearing from readers. Email me at ann@annroth.net, or write me c/o P.O. Box 25003, Seattle, WA 98165-1903, or visit my Facebook page. And please visit my website at www.annroth.net, where you can enter the monthly drawing to win a free book! You'll also find my latest writing news, tips for aspiring writers and a delicious new recipe every month.

The Rancher She Loved

ANN ROTH

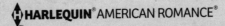

Recycling programs
for this product may
not exist in your area.

ISBN-13: 978-0-373-75460-1

THE RANCHER SHE LOVED

Printed in U.S.A.

ABOUT THE AUTHOR

Ann Roth lives in the greater Seattle area with her husband. After earning an MBA she worked as a banker and corporate trainer. She gave up the corporate life to write, and if they awarded PhDs in writing happily-ever-after stories, she'd surely have one.

Ann loves to hear from readers. You can write her at P.O. Box 25003, Seattle, WA 98165-1903 or email her at ann@annroth.net.

Books by Ann Roth

HARLEQUIN AMERICAN ROMANCE

*Saddlers Prairie

MRS. YANCY'S
DOUBLE CHOCOLATE DROP COOKIES

(with special thanks to *Country Fair Cookbook*)

Makes 2 to 4 dozen, depending on cookie size

6 oz (approximately 1 cup) semisweet chocolate pieces
1/2 cup softened butter
1/2 cup sugar
1 egg
1 cup flour
1/2 tsp baking soda
1/2 tsp salt
1/2 cup walnuts or pecans, chopped (optional)
6 oz (approximately 1 cup) semisweet chocolate pieces

Preheat oven to 350°F. Microwave 6 ounces of semisweet chocolate chips until melted; set aside to cool.

Cream together butter and sugar until light and fluffy. Add egg; beat well. Gradually add melted chocolate, beating well.

Mix together flour, baking soda and salt. Gradually add to creamed mixture and mix well. Stir in nuts and remaining chocolate chips. Drop by teaspoonfuls on greased baking sheets about 2 inches apart. (Mrs. Yancy prefers to use Silpat or parchment paper instead of greasing the cookie sheets.)

Bake 12 to 15 minutes or until done. Remove from baking sheets and cool on racks.

Chapter One

Sarah Tigarden drove down the deserted highway in the small ranching town of Saddlers Prairie, Montana, asking herself the question that would remain forever unanswered. Why hadn't her parents told her she was adopted?

Anger that had been with her since she'd discovered the truth welled, and the sunlit prairies on either side of the road seemed to dim.

Sarah didn't fault her father, who'd died when she was ten. But her mother, whom she now referred to as Ellen, could and should have told her. Now that she was gone, buried six months ago, it was too late.

They'd been close, growing closer still during the year before Ellen had succumbed to the ovarian cancer that ravaged her. Sarah had put her own life on hold, giving up her apartment and moving back home to care for Ellen. They'd talked about Sarah's recent breakup, finances, Ellen's burial—everything except the fact that Sarah was adopted.

She was still reeling from the shock that had awaited her when she'd emptied her mother's safe-deposit box. Surely Ellen had realized Sarah would find the birth certificate. She had to know how upset, how hurt Sarah would be. Not because of the adoption—because of the lies.

Why hadn't Ellen told the truth?

Sick of asking herself the question she might never find the answer to, Sarah cranked up the music and sang along with Adele. The words drowned out other thoughts, just as she wanted.

A sudden gust of wind sent dirt and debris flying, as if Mother Nature were upset on Sarah's behalf. Wind that pushed the car across the centerline. Gripping the wheel, Sarah steered her car to the right side of the road and fought to hold it there.

Ominous clouds suddenly obliterated the flawless blue sky that had been with her since she'd left Boise a day and a half earlier. Sarah tossed her sunglasses onto the passenger seat. Without the warmth of the mid-May sun, the temperature seemed to drop ten degrees, and she closed the sunroof and turned on the heat.

Maybe she should check in to her room first and change into warmer clothes. The widow who owned the house where she'd rented a room for the next two weeks was expecting her about now.

But that would involve a U-turn and a five-mile drive in the opposite direction, and Sarah was too anxious for answers. She wanted to know why Tammy Becker, her biological mother, had given her up, and where she was now. The private investigator Sarah had hired had tracked her mother to a house in Saddlers Prairie, where the Becker family had lived some twenty-nine years ago. It was there that the trail had abruptly ended— right around the time of Sarah's birth.

According to the P.I., a Mr. Tyler Phillips had bought the house from the Beckers all those years ago and still owned it. Unfortunately, his phone number was unlisted, and he hadn't answered either of the two letters Sarah had sent. If she showed up at his door, he'd be forced to at least talk to her. Maybe he'd share some valuable insights about Tammy Becker and her parents and provide information on where Tammy lived now. He might even let Sarah into the house. She wanted to walk through it, see Tammy's bedroom and gaze out the same windows her biological mother had once looked through.

She was curious. What kind of person was Tammy Becker, and had she ever thought about the daughter she'd given up? Sarah hoped to one day meet the woman and maybe even develop a relationship.

Even if Mr. Phillips refused to talk to her, she was determined to get some answers while she was in town. Following the directions on her iPhone GPS, she turned her travel-weary sedan onto a small paved street aptly named Dusty Horse Road.

Wouldn't you know, rain began to pummel the car and the dirt-packed ground, sending splashes of wet dust flying.

Great, just great.

The last time Sarah had visited Montana, to research an article on fly-fishing during a hot week in July a few years ago, she'd heard about the fickle spring climate. Now she was experiencing the abrupt shifts firsthand.

Her windshield wipers fought to keep pace with the downpour. Sarah slowed to a crawl, squinting through the weather at the numbers on the mailboxes.

They were few and far between, sentries at the feet of the driveways of modest homes. After a few minutes, the rain eased to a lighter, slower rhythm. She was beginning to wonder if she'd ever find the address she was looking for, when the GPS indicated the house she wanted was a few hundred feet away.

There it was—a bungalow situated back from the road, its pale green siding in need of fresh paint. Scraggly weeds filled the garden bed under the front window, but the large front and side yards were mowed, and buds filled the overgrown bushes along one side.

A black pickup was parked under a tall cottonwood at the edge of the gravel driveway. Someone was home—with any luck, Mr. Phillips himself.

This was it, the chance she'd hoped for. Slightly breathless, she pulled into the driveway and braked to a stop near the truck.

Shielding her hair with her shoulder bag, she dashed onto the porch, which was nothing but a concrete slab. Thanks to the overhang above the door, she was sheltered from the rain. Before ringing the doorbell, she smoothed her cap-sleeve blouse over her jeans and fluffed her hair, which had gotten wet despite the purse. Then she pressed the bell with a hand that trembled, thanks to a combination of nerves and a little fear. Though she couldn't have said what scared her.

Through the door she heard the faint, chiming *ding-dong*. Above her, clouds raced by, and another gust of wind whipped wet strands of hair across her face. So much for trying to look decent.

Sarah dug into her purse and quickly found her comb, but she needn't have hurried—Mr. Phillips, or whoever was inside, did not answer the door.

Maybe he needed extra time to reach it—the P.I. said he was in his mid-sixties—or maybe he hadn't heard the bell.

Determined, she rang again, letting her finger linger on the buzzer. After a short wait, she knocked. Nothing.

Frustrated and disappointed, but too curious to leave without at least sneaking a peek inside, she left the porch. Keeping under the shelter of the eaves, she stepped into the neglected garden along the front of the house.

Knee-high weeds raked the calves of her jeans, and mud sucked at her expensive leather slip-ons. Wishing she'd worn sneakers, she leaned forward and peered through the large front window into what appeared to be the living room. A sofa backed up against the window, and two armchairs and a coffee table faced an old TV. The off-white walls were completely bare. Mr. Phillips wasn't much for decorating.

Suddenly the deadbolt clicked. Sarah froze, but not for long. She turned and made a mad dash for the porch, stumbling over a dip in the ground in her haste. She'd barely regained her balance before the door swung open.

Caught in the garden like a thief. *Great way to make a first impression, Sarah.*

Her face burned, and she knew she was beet-red. With all the grace she could muster, she brushed off her hands and moved causally toward the door.

It wasn't until she planted her feet on the concrete slab that she mustered the courage to actually look at the large male standing in the doorway.

When she saw who it was, she almost stumbled again from the sheer shock. What was *Clay Hollyer* doing here?

The corner of his sexy mouth lifted in the devastating quirk women everywhere swooned over. Not Sarah— not anymore. She'd never thought she'd see him again and hadn't ever wanted to.

Yet there he was, as imposing and magnetic as ever. He pushed his longish brown hair off his forehead, momentarily exposing the faint scar along his right temple, the result of an angry bull's attempt to rid himself of his tenacious rider sometime during Clay's brilliant career as America's champion bull rider.

As talented and good-looking as he was, Clay Hollyer was also cocky and full of himself. He was one of the biggest players Sarah had ever met, let alone profiled for a magazine article. The buckle bunnies who buzzed around him, vying for his attention like bees around a honeycomb, only increased his inflated opinion of himself.

That Sarah had been one of them—not a buckle bunny, but just as smitten—made seeing him now all the worse.

It had been nearly three years. Plenty had happened since then, and she doubted he even remembered her. Hoped and prayed he didn't. But the striking jade eyes known to every rodeo fan in the world narrowed, and his lips compressed into a thin, flat line, and she knew that he did.

She wanted to sink into the ground. Or better yet, make a beeline for the car. But she was no coward. She forced a smile. "Hello, Clay. You probably don't remember me. I'm Sa—"

"Sarah Tigarden. How could I ever forget you?" His expression hardened, belying his light tone. "What the hell are you doing here?"

OF ALL THE women Clay had known, one of his least favorite was standing on his doorstep. If that wasn't bad enough, she'd trampled through the dead flower bed to snoop through the window.

He was so not amused.

Despite his nasty-ass scowl, she barely flinched. She

lost the phony smile though, and clutched the strap of her purse in a stranglehold. "I'm looking for Mr. Tyler Phillips."

"You want to talk my landlord." Clay snorted. "He doesn't live here, and FYI, he doesn't know anything about me."

"But this is his house."

"And he rented it to me. I don't do interviews anymore."

Even if he did, he wouldn't talk to her. A few years back, her big oh-so-guileless blue eyes and great legs had all but reeled him in. That and the habit she had of pushing her then long black hair behind her ears and catching her provocative lower lip between her teeth.

He'd soaked up her interest in him, had liked her enough that he'd even considered dating her. She didn't have the voluptuous curves he preferred, but those legs and her sweet little behind compensated for the small breasts.

Early one memorable morning, after ten days of letting her shadow him and answering her endless questions, he'd kissed her, in the stable with the horses, leaning against a clover-scented bale of hay. A sizzling kiss he'd thought about for months—and sometimes still did.

At the time, she'd seemed just as awed by the wallop that kiss had packed. Yet for some reason she'd cooled off, fast.

For the rest of the day and the night, she'd avoided being alone with him. The following morning, a full day before she was supposed to leave, she'd taken off without even thanking him for his time. She'd ignored his calls, emails and texts. Then she'd slammed him in print, calling him shallow, a player with a big ego that needed constant feeding. As if *he* were responsible for the women who threw themselves at him.

His buddies had laughed and said they wouldn't mind a similar article written about them, but that article had caused him no small amount of pain and trouble.

"I'm not here to do an interview, Clay."

Yeah, right. She was probably here to write a scathing piece about the life of a has-been. No, thanks.

Those big eyes widened, once more tempting him to fall under her spell and stay awhile. Not about to get suckered in again, he tore his gaze away. "How'd you find me?"

Not that his living here was a secret. He'd put out the press release himself, mostly to announce his new business venture. Since the accident and his forced retirement, interest from reporters had been all but nonexistent. Which suited him fine.

"Believe me, you're the last person I expected to run into," Sarah said. "I have no interest in you at all. None."

Why that bothered him was anyone's guess. She wasn't the first to feel that way. The angry bull that had crushed his knee had ruined more than his career. The buckle bunnies he'd once taken for granted had quickly turned their attention to other bull riders. Never mind that he'd driven them away. He didn't need their pity.

"Then why *are* you here?" he asked, not hiding his displeasure.

"I was hoping I could see the house."

Right, and he was a ballet dancer. "You're telling me Phillips wants to sell this place? Too bad—a couple of months ago, I signed a nine-month lease. I'm not leaving until the contractor finishes my house, and he just broke ground."

His bad leg was beginning to ache. He leaned against the doorjamb and crossed his arms.

"You're building a place in Saddlers Prairie." She frowned. "I thought you lived in Billings."

"I relocated."

"You're not riding anymore?"

She hadn't followed the stories, then. Just went to show how far he'd slipped from the radar. "Nope," he said. "I retired a year and a half ago."

The ache in his leg advanced to low-level pain, a sure sign that hell was on its way. He shouldn't have pushed himself so hard this morning.

"Thanks for stopping by." He backed inside and started to close the door.

"Wait—please!"

Her voice had a desperate ring to it he couldn't ignore. He hesitated.

"If I could just peek at the house," she said. "I won't stay long, I promise."

Vulnerability he hadn't noticed the last time they'd met made her look softer and even more attractive. Leaning heavily against the jamb, he eyed her. "Give me one good reason why I should believe you."

"How about the truth? I'm researching my family roots, and I found out that my mother and her parents once lived in this house."

He barely hid his surprise. "Can't you just ask them what you want to know?"

"I would, but both my parents are gone now—my adoptive parents, that is—and there are no other relatives to ask. This was my *biological* mother's house." Shadows filled her eyes. "Until recently, I didn't even know about her."

Interesting. "Closed adoption, huh?" he guessed.

"Something like that." She ducked her head, as if wanting to hide from him.

Curious, he cautiously flexed his bad leg. "When did she live here?"

"Twenty-nine years ago—when she was pregnant with me."

"And you're looking to learn something about her in this house, after all that time." Clay didn't buy it.

"I know it's a long shot, but it's all I have. Tyler Phillips bought this place from Bob and Judy Becker—my biological grandparents. The private investigator I hired said that Mr. Phillips still lived here. His phone number is unlisted, so I wrote to him for information, but he never replied. I thought that if I came in person, if he talked to me and showed me around, I might…never mind. Thanks for your time."

She turned away, but not before Clay saw her crestfallen expression.

Hell. He wasn't doing anything right now, anyway, so what could it hurt to let her in? "I'll give you ten minutes. Then you have to leave."

She brightened right up. "Thank you."

Chapter Two

Not knowing what to expect, Sarah followed Clay through the door. She couldn't help admiring his broad, straight back and wide shoulders, the way his jeans hung lovingly on his narrow hips and the powerful legs that were slightly bowed. Once, just once, she'd run her palms up his back and over his shoulders, while enjoying the kiss of her life. A huge mistake, she'd quickly learned.

He walked with a slight limp she didn't remember, probably from a bull-riding injury. She had no idea when that had happened, hadn't even realized he'd retired. But then, over the past year she'd barely had time to eat and write the articles that paid the bills, let alone keep up with what was new on the rodeo circuit.

"You've seen the living room," he said, his deadpan face more expressive than any dirty look. "Kitchen's this way."

With its worn yellow linoleum and blue-and-white tiled counters, the small kitchen looked original. Sarah's excitement mounted. A built-in table and two benches filled a windowed nook that faced the big backyard.

She tried to picture Tammy and her parents eating there. Having no idea what they looked like made imagining them difficult.

"You're staring at the table like you expect it to talk," Clay said.

"It looks like it's been there a long time, and I was thinking about Tammy—my biological mother—sitting there."

His hands on the counter behind him, Clay regarded her solemnly. "What do you know about the Becker family?"

"Not much, except that at some point after Tammy got pregnant, her parents sold the house to Mr. Phillips. She was sixteen."

"My mom was eighteen when she got pregnant with me."

Sarah nodded. "Your parents got married the day after they graduated from high school, about five months before you were born. And they're still married."

"You remember that, huh?"

The corner of his mouth lifted, making him oh, so appealing, and she had to glance away. "You're lucky they didn't give you up, and that they didn't hide their past from you. I only learned the truth six months ago."

She wasn't sure why she told him. Probably because despite his initial hostility, he listened as if what she said mattered. It was one of the qualities that had first attracted her to him. He'd no doubt discovered that women were drawn to a man who paid attention.

"I guess I was lucky," he said. "If my folks had given me up and separated, I wouldn't have a sister and brother-in-law or two nieces."

"You have a second niece now?"

"Fiona. She's almost two, and a real pistol. And my parents did hide the truth from me. They never told me squat about their shotgun wedding. My aunt is the one who spilled the beans, to get back at my mom for something or other. After that, they didn't speak for years."

She hadn't known that. Clay rubbed his leg above the knee and winced.

"Your leg hurts," she observed.

"It's fine." He straightened and gingerly flexed his knee. "You don't know where the Beckers went?"

He seemed genuinely interested, and Sarah wanted to talk about it. She'd told her friends back home everything she knew, mulling over what-ifs and possibilities ad nauseum, and they'd quickly grown tired of the subject. They didn't even think she should be here, thought she should forget all about Tammy Becker and get on with her life.

Sarah agreed, and once she learned the answers to her questions, she intended to do just that. She shook her head. "They seem to have vanished."

"I hope you find them."

"You and me both."

His eyes beamed warmth and sympathy, making him all but irresistible. Her stomach flip-flopped just as it had the day she'd first met him in person and seen how his high-wattage grin caused the corners of his eyes to crinkle.

All right, she was attracted to him, had fallen a little in love with him three years ago. At the time, she'd stupidly thought he felt something, too. Ha. She'd quickly realized that any interest Clay had shown her was short-lived. He didn't really want to get to know her for who she was—or any other woman, for that matter.

It hadn't taken long for her to discover that, aside from bull riding, Clay Hollyer specialized in playing the field. No doubt, he probably still did.

Which was why she wasn't going to pay any attention

to the feelings flirting with her insides. She was only drawn to Clay because, for one thing, he was gorgeous, and for another, she hadn't been with a man since she and Matthew had broken up over a year ago. Between caring for her mother and her freelance magazine work, Sarah simply hadn't had time for a boyfriend and had ended the relationship.

She wasn't about to let Clay's charm and good looks affect her pulse rate—even if she did dream about him from time to time. Steamy dreams that led to restless nights.

The past few months, she'd all but banished him from her thoughts. And now here she was, standing in his house, fighting those same feelings. "Shall we continue with the tour?" she asked in a far cooler tone.

In a blink, the warmth disappeared from his eyes and his expression blanked. He nodded toward the hallway beyond the kitchen. "Head back down the hall."

As she turned and exited the room, she swore she felt his gaze on her rear end. Resisting the urge to tug her blouse over her hips, she gestured for him to lead the way. Instead, he fell into step beside her. The hallway was barely wide enough to accommodate them both.

Familiar smells she thought she'd forgotten teased her senses—the clean soap Clay used, and underneath, his masculine scent. Edging closer to the wall, she trained her gaze on the worn carpet.

"There isn't much to this house—just the kitchen, living room, bathroom and two bedrooms," he said.

Struggling with herself to pay attention to the house instead of the man beside her, she managed an interested nod.

What was the matter with her? She'd come here to find out what she could about Tammy Becker and her parents, not dredge up the one-sided emotions she'd once felt for Clay Hollyer.

"This is where I sleep," he said, pointing to a bedroom. The bed was unmade, the covers thrown back. "The house came furnished, but I brought my own king-size bed. I like to stretch out and get comfy."

Sarah just bet he did. Images of wild sex all over that bed filled her head. She glanced around the room without really taking in the furnishings. "May I see the other bedroom?"

"Sure. It's right across the hall." He opened the closed door of the second bedroom and stood back for her to pass.

This room was smaller, and the air smelled stale. A twin bed stood against the wall, much like the one still in Sarah's bedroom at Ellen's house. Judging by the yellowing striped wallpaper that curled along the seams, the flowery bedspread and lacy pillows that looked as outdated as the faded pink curtains, the decor hadn't been changed in ages. No wonder Clay kept the door closed.

Obviously, this had been a girl's bedroom. A white desk and wicker chair, the kind a teen might use to do homework, faced a window that overlooked the backyard.

Sarah sucked in a breath. "Do you think this room is the same as it was when Tammy lived here?"

"I wouldn't know, but why would the family leave the furniture behind when they moved?"

Sarah had no idea. "It's awfully girlie and really dated. I wonder why Mr. Phillips never stripped the wallpaper, or at least replaced the bedding and curtains."

"Maybe he likes pink. Tour's over."

Sarah wasn't sure what she'd expected, but she hadn't anticipated even more unanswerable questions. She let out a disappointed sigh. "Thanks for letting me come in."

In the hallway, something made her glance up. A short pull rope hung from a door in the ceiling. "Is that an attic?"

"Probably."

"You haven't been up there?" When Clay shook his head, she said, "Could I take a peek?"

"Some other time." His mouth settled into a grim line.

He wanted her gone. Sarah understood—she was uncomfortable around him, too. Yet some sixth sense told her that she might find something important in the attic. If only she could talk with Mr. Phillips…

"I'd like to ask Mr. Phillips about the Beckers," she said. "Would you mind giving me his number?"

Clay shrugged one shoulder and supplied it as she input the information into her phone. "You won't be able to reach him, though," he said. "He doesn't own a cell, and right now he and his wife are someplace in Europe."

That explained why he hadn't answered her letters. "Does he have an email address?"

"Nope."

"When will he be back?"

"In the fall."

Her hopes plummeted. "If he contacts you, will you let him know I'd like to talk? Here's my contact information." She handed Clay her card.

Without a glance, he slid it into his hip pocket. "How long are you in town?"

"Two weeks."

"That's a long time to search for your biological mom

who probably lives someplace else. Besides ranching, there isn't much to do around here. If I were you, I'd leave a lot sooner."

He *really* wanted her gone.

Not about to let him intimidate her, she pulled herself up tall. "Actually, I'm also here to research and write an article on ranching life in Montana. I only hope two weeks is enough."

Clay's face was unreadable. "Interviewing anyone in particular? I'll warn them to watch out for you."

"What does that mean?" Sarah asked, though she knew.

"It means that you act all sweet and caring about a guy and then you trash him in a magazine story."

She *had* cared, and thought he cared, too. Especially when, a few days before she was leaving, he'd kissed her. Not just a little peck, but a long, heady kiss filled with feeling and promise. Even now she remembered the hot flare of desire inside her, and the certainty that standing in the warmth of his arms was exactly where she belonged.

Some scant hours later, while sitting in the bleachers, watching a crew set up for an upcoming rodeo, she'd overheard two buckle bunnies nearby.

"I had sex with Clay last night," said the one with *the fake red hair and size double-D breasts.*

"Way to go." Her friend had high-fived her. *"Is he as good as they say?"*

"The best I've ever had. But don't trust me, knock on his door tonight and find out for yourself."

Sarah raised her chin. "Everything in that article was true."

Clay's expression darkened, and he swore. "I'm not

shallow and my ego isn't that big. You spent ten whole days with me, Sarah. You know that."

He was and it was, but she wasn't going to stand there and argue. She wanted to get far, far away from Clay, and forget all about him. If he would just let her look around the attic…

She glanced up. "Let me see what's up there, and then I promise I'll go."

Clay checked his watch. "We agreed that you'd leave after ten minutes, yet you've been here for over thirty."

That long? "I can't shake the feeling that there might be something up there of Tammy's," she said. "Please."

Clay blew out an exasperated breath. "Don't tell me you're going to pull that again."

Having no idea what he meant, she frowned. "Excuse me?"

"Making your eyes extra big and biting your bottom lip."

"I don't know what you're talking about. One look around the attic is all I ask. Then I'll go, and you'll never see me again."

"Is that a promise?"

Sarah bit back a retort, which wouldn't help. "You won't have to do a thing. Just point me to a stepladder and I'll take care of the rest."

He muttered something about her stubbornness.

"You're right," she said. "When I want something, I *am* stubborn."

"Will you quit doing that?"

She was biting her bottom lip again, she realized. She rolled her eyes and forced a smile. "Is this better?"

"Unfortunately, no."

He advanced toward her with an intent expression she felt clear to her toes.

Swallowing, she stepped back. "The stepladder?"

"I think there's one in the utility room," Clay said, moving closer still.

Her heart pounding, Sarah retreated another step, but the wall stopped her. "I-is it off the kitchen?"

"You're driving me crazy," he said in a low voice, and leaned in even closer.

"Clay, I don't—"

He silenced her with a kiss.

CLAY DIDN'T TRUST Sarah, didn't want her there and sure as hell shouldn't go near her. But there was something about her he couldn't resist.

Her eyes were huge and a little scared, but as soon as he brushed his mouth over hers, the look in them softened and her eyelids drifted closed.

Clay also closed his eyes. Her perfume, flowery and as fresh as a spring day, was different from before, but every bit as seductive. She'd cut her hair short, but it felt just as silky as when it had reached her shoulders.

If there were other differences, he didn't sense them. She felt good in his arms, tasted sweet.

Just as he remembered.

With the little sigh he'd been waiting for without realizing it, she gave in and kissed him back. Her hands slid up his arms and wrapped around his neck, bringing her soft breasts tight against his chest.

Wanting to get closer, he shifted his weight. Wrong move. His leg screamed, snapping him out of his haze of desire.

What was he doing? Was he *nuts?* He dropped his hands and stepped back.

Looking slightly unfocused, Sarah tugged at her blouse. "Why did you do that?"

Because he hadn't been able to stop himself. "I wanted to find out if you tasted as good as I remember," he drawled. "And you do."

Good enough that for a brief time he'd forgotten the searing pain in his knee. He needed to pop four extra-strength aspirin *now,* and then prop up his leg.

Not in front of Sarah. It was only out of sheer will-power that he managed to stay on his feet.

She as good as ran for the door.

Gritting his teeth, he strode after her and banged it open in time to let her out. "Goodbye, Sarah Tigarden."

She left without a backward glance.

MRS. YANCY, THE sixty-something grandmotherly widow Sarah had rented a room from, seemed glad for the company. When Sarah returned from putting her things in the bedroom up a narrow set of stairs, her temporary landlady showed her around her colorful house, pointing out treasures she'd collected. She liked primary colors and flowers, and the fabrics of the drapes and furniture were filled with both. An eclectic selection of pictures and wall hangings decorated most of the wall space, and knickknacks crowded every available table and windowsill.

The woman herself was just as bright and energetic, and a whole lot friendlier than Clay.

But Sarah wasn't going to think about him—even if she was still reeling from that kiss. A kiss every bit as potent as the ones she remembered.

What really rattled her, though, was that she'd enjoyed every moment of it so much. The hard strength of his arms, the delicious press of his mouth...

"The washer and dryer are behind those corded doors," Mrs. Yancy said just before they entered a modest but homey kitchen. "You're on your own for lunch and dinner, and if you want to cook your own meals, feel free to use the kitchen. You will get breakfast every morning. I hope you like eggs and biscuits. I didn't know if you drank coffee or tea, so I stocked up on both."

She clasped her hands at her ample waist, as if anxious for Sarah's approval.

No one had cooked for Sarah in ages, and she relished the thought. "Eggs and biscuits sound delicious, and I'm a coffee drinker."

"So am I, but if you decide you want tea, there's a sampler box in the cabinet above the stove. Which reminds me—for groceries, head to Spenser's General Store, about seven miles up the highway. You'll find just about anything you might want there, including prepared food. If you'd rather eat out, Barb's Café is right next door to Spenser's. It's our only real restaurant, and the food is excellent. We also have pizza and fast-food places."

Sarah mentally stored away the information.

"If you have questions about anything at all, don't hesitate to ask," Mrs. Yancy continued.

Maybe the woman had known the Beckers. "Have you lived in Saddlers Prairie long?" Sarah asked.

"Almost twenty-five years. After John and I married, I moved here from Ely, Nevada. He was my second husband. The first one didn't work out." Briefly, her smile dimmed. "I'll bet you've never heard of Ely."

The woman jumped subjects like a leaping frog. "No, I haven't," Sarah said.

"It's on the east side of the state. I met John when he came through town, offering insurance policies to ranchers. His home was Saddlers Prairie, so this is where we settled.

"At first, it seemed awfully small—even smaller than Ely. I didn't know a soul besides my husband, and with him out and about, selling insurance to ranchers all over the West, I was afraid I'd get homesick. But the folks around here reached out to me, and in no time, I felt as if I'd lived here all my life. John's been gone eight years now, and my friends here treat me like family. I've never spent a birthday or holiday alone."

Now that Ellen was gone, Sarah wondered how she'd spend the holidays. Not that she didn't have friends, but they had their own families.

"This sounds like a very special place," she said. Even though Mrs. Yancy had arrived in Saddlers Prairie after the Beckers had sold their home, you never knew. "Did you by chance ever meet a family named Becker?"

The widow glanced at the ceiling, thinking, and then shook her head. "Not that I recall. But why don't you join me over coffee and the oatmeal cookies I baked this morning, and I'll think on it some more."

At the mention of food, Sarah salivated. In the anxiety and excitement over seeing the house where the Beckers had once lived, her appetite had all but vanished, and she hadn't eaten much breakfast or lunch. "That sounds wonderful," she said.

Minutes later, she was sharing the kitchen table with her talkative landlady, two steaming mugs of coffee and a plate of chewy cookies.

"You never said why you've come to Saddlers Prairie," Mrs. Yancy said.

"One reason is to do research for an article on ranching in eastern Montana."

"I had no idea you were a writer." She looked impressed. "It's about time somebody sang the praises of Saddlers Prairie. I enjoy reading magazines. Which one do you write for?"

"I freelance for several." Sarah listed them. "One of the editors who buys my pieces thought an article on ranching would appeal to her readers. I love the idea, and since I wanted to look around here, anyway, I happily accepted the assignment. I hope to meet with successful ranchers, but also those who are struggling, so that I can paint a realistic picture. Anything you can share about Saddlers Prairie will be a big help."

"I'll keep that in mind. You say you also want to look around town?"

"That's right." Sarah saw no reason to hide the truth. "I was adopted, but I recently learned that I was born in Saddlers Prairie."

"No kidding. I know just about everyone. Who are your kin?"

"They don't live around here anymore, but their last name is Becker—Bob and Judy."

"The people you asked about."

Sarah nodded. "They may have left the area before you arrived. I know they sold their house here about twenty-nine years ago."

"There are folks in town who've been here longer than that. Someone will surely know the family you're looking for." Mrs. Yancy sipped her coffee. "I'll ask around and see what I can find out."

"Would you?" Fresh hope bubbled through Sarah. "I really want to know the kind of people I come from."

"I understand." The landlady looked thoughtful. "Over my sixty-six years of living, I've learned a few things." She leaned forward and lowered her voice, as if she were about to divulge a secret. "One of the most important, which my John taught me, is that who you are matters more than your people or where you came from."

Sarah wasn't sure she agreed. "I still need to know," she said. "If you were standing in my shoes, wouldn't you?"

"I suppose so. I wish I could help." She looked genuinely sorry.

"You already have," Sarah said. "By listening to my story."

Clay had listened, too, with just as much interest.

She wished she could stop thinking about him. When she'd dated Matthew, she'd all but managed to forget Clay, and she wasn't about to waste her time pining for him again.

If only he hadn't kissed her.

A long and very thorough kiss that had stolen her breath and chased away her common sense. For those few moments, she'd been right back where she was three years ago, caring too much, too quickly for a man who couldn't be trusted.

"—know a few ranchers around here who fit what you're looking for and would love to be interviewed for your article," Mrs. Yancy was saying. "If you want, I'll give you names. There's a pen and paper in the catch-all drawer under the phone."

As soon as Sarah returned with the writing supplies, the woman rattled off the names, addresses and phone numbers of two ranchers. By heart.

"You'll definitely want to contact Dawson Ranch," she said. "Adam and Drew Dawson own about the most successful ranch around. Now the Lucky A Ranch isn't as profitable, but Lucky Arnett is a good man with plenty of stories about his life as a rancher. I don't want you to get writers' cramp so I'll save the rest for later."

Smiling at the little joke, Sarah flexed her fingers and traded the pen for her mug. After months of grief and anger, Mrs. Yancy's warmth and friendliness were like a balm to her parched soul.

"Wait—there is one more person you might want to talk with," the older woman said. "He's a celebrity with star power the world over, and he's chosen Saddlers Prairie as his new home. I'm sure you've heard of him—his name is Clay Hollyer."

Sarah almost choked on her coffee. "As a matter of fact, I know Clay. I interviewed him for an article a few years ago."

Mrs. Yancy looked both impressed and curious. Not about to answer any questions about that time, Sarah hurried on. "Funny thing. Earlier this afternoon, when I first arrived in town, I stopped at the house where the Beckers used to live. The man who bought it from them still owns it, and I hoped to talk with him. It turns out, he doesn't live there. He rented the house to Clay."

"I know that place, and I know Ty Phillips. He runs the lumber company outside town, and has for years. I don't think he lived in that house for long. Shelley wanted something brand-new, and after they married, he custom-built her a real nice home. Right now, they're in Europe, taking a long-overdue vacation."

"That's what Clay said. So that house has always been a rental?"

"Since I've lived here. Mind you, Ty hasn't always been able to find a renter. From time to time the place has stood empty. Even so, he's managed to keep it in pretty decent condition.

"Back to Clay. He just bought the old Bates Ranch, a

neglected ranch on the other side of town, and renamed it Hollyer Ranch. The main house there was in particularly bad shape, and he had it torn down. Now he's building his own custom house and working on plans to start up a stock contracting business."

Clay had mentioned building a house but hadn't said a word about buying a ranch or beginning a new career. But then, Sarah hadn't asked. His life seemed to have changed drastically from the spotlighted fame of before.

"I'm not sure I know what a stock contractor is," she said.

"Those are the folks who supply stock—bulls, steers and horses—to rodeos around the country. A good business for a man who knows his bulls, as Clay does, wouldn't you say? You should probably interview him, too."

Oh, that would go over well. He'd probably slam the door in her face—or worse. Sarah managed a smile. "Thanks for the lead, but I'll stick with ranchers who've been in business for a while."

Chapter Three

As always, Clay awoke around 4:00 a.m., a good hour and change ahead of the birds. He'd had a bad night, and rolled over and tried to fall back into dreamland. But his mind wouldn't cooperate, and thoughts buzzed in and out of his head like pesky gnats.

Groaning, he flipped onto his back. Before the accident, he'd always slept like the dead. Now, no matter how late he turned in or how tired he was, he woke up at this ungodly hour.

Propping his arms behind his head, he stared up into the darkness. And thought about Sarah. That kiss.

He still couldn't believe she'd shown up at his door with her story and those big eyes, or that he'd let her in. If she'd just gone away when he asked her to. She'd had to ruin everything by stubbornly insisting she wanted to see the attic.

He wasn't about to let her up there and wasn't about to check it out himself, either. Not even to erase her pleading look. With his leg in the sorry shape it was, climbing a ladder would be agony.

Did she have a boyfriend? Probably, and if he found out about that kiss, he'd go ballistic. Clay would.

In any event, it had done its job, chasing her away. There was only one little problem—Clay hadn't figured on the restless energy and hunger that kiss had stirred up, making him want what he had no business even thinking about. Sarah, naked under him, flushed and passionate.

He scoffed. Like that would ever happen. She thought he was a player.

"I'm no player," he insisted into the silence. "I'm a straightforward guy who likes women." What the hell was wrong with that?

Before he'd started winning bull-riding contests and making serious money, he'd even worked at building a solid relationship with the thought that it might lead to marriage. Denise had been too impatient, though. She'd wanted to get married right away, and when Clay wasn't ready to commit, she'd walked. Same issue with Hailey, and a couple of years later, with Cara.

After striking out three times, Clay had finally figured out the problem. He'd been infatuated with his girlfriends, but nothing more. Not counting his mom, sister, aunt and grandmothers, he'd never loved a woman, and probably never would.

So he dated casually. He never led a woman on, always admitted up front that he was interested in having a good time, period.

"If that makes me a player," he muttered, "then so be it."

Sarah hadn't even paid him the courtesy of checking out the facts. God knew where she'd gotten the cockeyed idea that he went around lying to women and breaking hearts.

Her article had brought a whole host of women to his door, most of them interested in grabbing some of his fame and money for themselves. Jeanne had been the worst of the bunch. She was cute and seemed nice enough. Clay had dated her on and off, making sure she understood that their relationship was casual and that he was dating other women, as well. She didn't seem to mind.

Then a few hours before what turned out to be his last rodeo, after they hadn't seen each other for a good six weeks, she'd shown up and announced that she was pregnant and he was responsible. Having always used protection, Clay had his doubts, but Jeanne swore that he was the only man she'd been intimate with.

It was not the kind of news a man needed to hear before a nationally televised bull ride with a six-figure purse. As upset and distracted as Clay was, he should've backed out of the event. He didn't. Not because of the money, which he didn't need, but because of his fans. He hadn't wanted to disappoint them.

No wonder the bull had tossed him.

While he was still recuperating in the hospital, he'd insisted on a paternity test. No surprise there—he wasn't the father.

Grumbling and out of sorts, he swung his legs over the bed without thinking—and paid for it. Swearing, he massaged the knots around his knee until the pain eased and carefully stood. His leg muscles were painfully tight, but thank heavens, not quite as tight as yesterday. Aspirin and rest had definitely helped.

While the coffee brewed, he pulled out the blueprints for the house and looked them over. After making the decision to buy the shipwreck of a ranch across town and rent the house he was in now, he'd hired a construction crew to renovate the ranch's outbuildings and an architect to help him design his house. Now that the old one was gone and the builder had broken ground, Clay enjoyed reviewing the plans and checking on the progress.

Four bedrooms and three-and-a-half baths seemed a lot for a man who didn't intend to have a family. Clay had always wanted kids, but he couldn't see having one without a wife, and he wasn't about to marry without love. Even if his mom kept dropping hints—make that blatant suggestions—that now that he was thirty-four it was time to settle down.

Before long, the caffeine worked its magic. Clay shoved to his feet, stowed the blueprints and headed for the large detached garage behind the house, which was insulated and had electricity, making it the ideal place for physical therapy.

After being shackled to a leg cast for what seemed an eternity and spending months in a wheelchair, his leg was in sorry shape, and laboring to rebuild his strength was not fun. The repetitive efforts the physical therapist had taught him taxed his leg muscles until they burned.

A hundred times over the next hellish hour, Clay wanted to quit, but he kept at it. Determined to get back to normal, or as near normal as possible, he sweated, grunted at and cursed the weights and pulleys, all the while knowing that without them, the muscles that had deteriorated would never regain their strength.

To think that two months after the accident, his doctor had wanted to amputate above the knee. Clay had refused. In the past eight months he'd made amazing progress, graduating from the wheelchair to crutches to a cane to none of the above, blowing his orthopedist's socks off.

"And I'll keep blowing your mind, Doc," he'd stated, to psych himself up.

By the time he showered, dressed and ate, it was just

after six o'clock—the start of a typical rancher's work-day. As of yet, he didn't have a crew, but now that the barn and outbuildings were renovated and the foreman's cottage and crew trailers were clean, he'd posted an ad on Craigslist for experienced ranch hands. He didn't own any stock yet, either, and time hung like a weight around his neck.

Feeling lost and as a rudderless boat, he wandered to the hallway that held the attic door. Until yesterday he'd never even considered going up there. May as well test the leg, and while he did, look around.

With the help of a stepladder and several colorful oaths, he gritted his teeth against the pain and grasped the rope pull. The thing resisted coming loose but Clay yanked hard, and the door swung down.

He unfolded the attic ladder and climbed up, pausing after each step to rest his leg. The usual attic greeted him—a musty-smelling, dingy space, cold from the chilly morning air. A lone window caked in grime and a bare bulb hanging in the middle of the ceiling were the only sources of light and barely illuminated the area.

In need of a flashlight or a bulb with higher wattage, he headed back down, ignoring his leg. In no time, he was screwing in a new bulb.

Light blazed over the room, revealing old lamps, a faded armchair and other junk, everything blanketed with dust.

He almost missed the footlocker in the corner. Shoved against the wall, it was partially hidden under a musty throw. Clay unfastened the clasps and tried the lid, gratified when it opened with a soft creak.

Papers and whatnot almost filled the cavity. The *16 Magazine* on top caught his attention. Duran Duran posed on the cover, flashing '80s-style hair and clothes—something a teen girl would like. The date on the cover was January, 1982, which was when Tammy Becker had lived here.

Beneath the magazine, Clay found a small, dark red journal covered in faux leather. *Private diary! Stay out! T. B.* someone had written. Judging by the hearts replacing periods and the looping script, T.B. was a teenage girl.

This footlocker belonged to Sarah's biological mom. That sixth sense of hers had been dead-on.

A chill climbed his neck.

No snoop, Clay closed the lid and refastened the latches. He dragged the heavy trunk from the corner, the metal grating over the rough floorboards and his damn knee threatening to buckle.

Grunting with effort, he hugged the big thing with one arm and awkwardly made his way down the ladder. By the time he reached the floor, sweat beaded his forehead and he was breathing like he'd just gone a round with a feisty bull.

Sarah's card was still in the hip pocket of his jeans. Leaning heavily against the wall, Clay slid it out and held it lightly in his palm. At this hour, she was probably still asleep. He'd wait awhile, and then give her a call.

AFTER A SOLID night's sleep, Sarah felt more rested than she had in ages. She donned a robe and flip-flops and wandered downstairs in search of coffee. Even before she reached the bottom step, she smelled bacon and something baking. Still waking up, she wasn't hungry yet. All the same her mouth watered.

Standing at the stove, dressed, aproned and humming happily, Mrs. Yancy greeted her with a welcoming smile. "Good morning. It's going to be a beautiful day. The biscuits are in the oven."

"They sure smell good. So does that coffee." Sarah stretched and yawned.

"Help yourself, dear, and sit down. Was your bed comfortable? Did you have enough blankets?"

After sleeping in the twin bed of her childhood for over a year—Sarah couldn't get herself to use the bed that had been Ellen's—the double bed here had seemed a luxury. "Everything was great, thanks. Your neighborhood is very peaceful."

So was Ellen's street in Boise, but since her death, Sarah rarely slept through the night. Her friends thought she should put the house on the market and buy a condo or a cottage, something without the memories. Sarah agreed, but if she wanted a good price for the property, both the house and the yard needed sprucing up—tasks she would tackle later. "It's not so peaceful with all those chirping birds outside," Mrs. Yancy said. "Between the warblers, sparrows and crows, it's impossible for a body to sleep past dawn. Not that I ever have. Breakfast will be ready shortly."

Slipping on oven mitts, she launched into a monologue about her bird feeder and the types of birds that visited. Her words barely slowed as she pulled the biscuits from the oven and deftly transferred them to a basket.

Sarah didn't mind the chatter, as long as she didn't have to participate. She needed a moment to sip her coffee and get her mind up and running. Thankfully, Mrs. Yancy seemed content to carry on the entire conversation by herself, reminding Sarah of Ellen.

Her mother was the last person she wanted to think about right now. As angry as she was about the lies, she missed Ellen dearly. If only she were still around and they could argue and cry and talk through this whole mess and move on…

Abruptly Mrs. Yancy's chatter died. "You look sad, dear."

"I was thinking about Ellen—my mother. She died six months ago. Do you need help with breakfast?"

"No, but go ahead and grab a plate from the cabinet and dish up your eggs and bacon at the stove. I'm sorry about your mother. Were you close?"

Not as close as Sarah had thought. "Most of the time," she said.

"It's good that you put off the search to find your biological mother until now. This way, your actual mother can't get upset at what you're doing."

Having filled her plate, Sarah sat down at the table. "How could looking for my biological mother possibly have upset Ellen?"

"It just can." Mrs. Yancy didn't say another word until she brought over the biscuits and her own plate and sat down across the table. She let out a sigh. "I was terribly upset when my son decided to search for his biological mother."

Sarah masked her surprise. Had Mrs. Yancy also kept the truth from her son, and if so, what were her reasons? How had he discovered the truth? Those and a thousand other questions came to mind, yet as open and easy as her breakfast companion was to talk to, Sarah didn't know her well enough to ask such personal things. "Does your son live in town?" she asked, settling for a harmless enough question.

"Sadly, no. Tom lives in Billings with his wife and their three kids. He's a good son. I visit them several times a year, and they come here now and then, but we don't see each other nearly often enough."

She turned her attention to her breakfast for a few moments before continuing. "He was twenty when he decided he wanted to reunite with his biological mother. She lives in Albuquerque. I'm embarrassed to admit this now, but at the time, I worried that he'd choose her over me. My John assured me otherwise, but all the same, I lost many a night's sleep."

Sarah had never even considered such a possibility. "How did it all work out?" she asked.

"Tom's biological mother was thrilled to hear from him. She'd gotten pregnant at fifteen and knew she wasn't ready to give him the stability and family he needed, but she'd always wanted to know him. She'd gone on to college, where she met her husband. They have two children—Tom has met the entire family.

"From time to time they talk on the phone, and once in a while they see each other, but I'm the one Tom visits on Mother's Day. He says I nursed him when he was sick, hollered at him when he needed it and helped him with his schoolwork, and that makes me his *real* mother."

"I never even thought about any of that," Sarah admitted. Now that Mrs. Yancy had opened up, she felt safe asking a question. "What made Tom decide to find his biological mother? Had he just found out that he was adopted?"

"Heavens, no. We talked about that from the time he was old enough to understand—even before then. We always celebrated his adoption day with a cake and presents. He just wanted to meet her."

Sarah chewed a forkful of eggs, then voiced her own

question. "How did your family celebrate your adoption day?"

"We didn't." Ducking her head from the woman's questioning look, Sarah slathered a biscuit with jam.

Comprehension, then sympathy dawned on Mrs. Yancy's face. "Your mother never told you."

Sarah shook her head. "I don't even know if it was a closed adoption. I couldn't find any paperwork. I just wish I knew why she kept something so important from me."

"I'm sure she had her reasons."

Whatever they were, Sarah would never know. She hoped Tammy Becker could shed some light on the matter.

"Your biological mother probably doesn't know your actual mother's reasons for keeping the adoption secret," Mrs. Yancy said as if she'd read Sarah's mind. "She probably never met your mother."

"No, but they may have exchanged letters."

Sarah hoped. She hadn't found any, but her mother had been a no-nonsense woman who liked a tidy house. She'd never been the type to save things. Or maybe she'd simply disposed of any correspondence so Sarah wouldn't accidentally find it. But then, why leave the birth certificate in her safe-deposit box?

Sarah wanted answers, *needed* them, in order to make sense of things. So that she could at least gain some insight into why her mother had kept the adoption a secret.

"Are there any family members you could ask—grandparents or cousins?" Mrs. Yancy said.

"No."

"What about friends of your parents?"

"I asked my mother's best friend, her church friends

and the women from her bridge club. Not a single person knew that I was adopted. My parents moved to Boise when I was a baby, and I guess the subject never came up."

Another baffling shock Sarah couldn't get over. Keeping such a huge secret from even your most trusted friends seemed unimaginable and beyond comprehension.

Why?

The question reverberated through her head as it had for months, making her crazy with the what-ifs that circled right back to the original question.

Why?

Weary of that dead-end question, she broached a different subject. "I thought I'd call the Dawson brothers and Lucky Arnett today and set up interviews. I'm also planning to explore the area. Should I get a key so that I don't have to bother you with my coming and going?"

"No need—I never lock my door. Well, that's not quite true. When I leave town, I do."

Clay Hollyer kept his door locked. Sarah remembered the loud click of the deadbolt as he slid it back. "Even in quiet, safe Boise, we lock our doors," she said.

"Here, most of us don't. Although there are people who lock their doors for one reason or another."

No doubt, Clay didn't want any nosy reporters walking into his house. Which was exactly what he'd taken her for.

"The Tates, my next-door neighbors, started locking their door last summer." Mrs. Yancy dived into a comical story of the time Mr. Tate's unwanted relatives showed up and made themselves comfortable while the couple was out for the day. Which led into a story of another friend's cow, which somehow figured out how to open the gate to the back garden.

In no time, the amusing stories pushed all thoughts of Ellen from Sarah's mind.

She laughed and let out an inward sigh of relief. When the meal ended, she was still smiling.

AFTER BREAKFAST, MRS. YANCY refused Sarah's offer to help clean up. "You're a paying guest, and you're not supposed to do the breakfast dishes," she said. "But you can sit and keep me company awhile longer."

Mrs. Yancy suggested places to see in the area. Sarah was at the table, jotting down notes, when her cell phone rang.

Private caller, the screen said, and she almost let it go to voice mail. But she never had been good at ignoring calls. What if an editor with a blocked number was calling about an assignment? She picked up. "This is Sarah Tigarden."

"It's Clay."

The deep, slightly gruff voice sounded rusty, as if he'd just awakened. Sarah pictured him in a T-shirt and rumpled pair of pajama bottoms, his hair sticking up and stubble on his face.

Her heart fluttered and her whole body warmed. Shifting nervously, she glanced at Mrs. Yancy, who was busy wiping down the stove. As if the older woman could save her from her unwanted feelings.

Schooling her wayward emotions, she managed a cool, "Hello, Clay. What do you want?"

A rude question, but she needed him to understand that she hadn't asked for and didn't appreciate that kiss.

Okay, that was so not true.

Mrs. Yancy's head whipped around, her eyebrows rising comically up her forehead.

Clay cleared his throat, as if the question threw him. "I was up in the attic this morning."

He'd found something. Sarah gripped the phone. "Oh?" she said, barely masking her excitement.

"I don't know how you knew to check the attic, but I've got a footlocker here that I'm pretty sure belonged to Tammy."

Her heart pounded loudly in her ears. "You found a footlocker that probably belonged to Tammy," she paraphrased for Mrs. Yancy's benefit. "When can I take a look at it?"

"This morning is good."

Moments later, she disconnected. "I'll make those calls to the ranchers later. I'm going back to Clay's to see that footlocker."

"Don't you think you should put on some clothes first?" Behind her bifocals, Mrs. Yancy's eyes twinkled.

In her eagerness, Sarah had forgotten she was still in her robe and pajamas. "Right. Excuse me while I shower and dress."

Some thirty minutes later, wearing her favorite jeans, the ones that flattered her rear end, she headed downstairs. Mrs. Yancy was waiting for her in the living room.

"You're wearing makeup, and the royal blue color of that blouse brings out the blue in your eyes and the roses in your cheeks. Clay is sure to notice how pretty you are."

Sarah blushed. "I'm not interested in him." At least, she didn't want to be. She felt compelled to add, "This is how I usually dress—except for days like yesterday, when I was on the road, traveling."

"Well, you look lovely. I'll be interested to know what you find in that footlocker."

"I'll let you know," Sarah said. "I'm not sure when I'll be back."

"No worries. If I'm not here, walk on in and make yourself at home."

Grateful for the woman's trust and kindness, Sarah smiled and hurried out the door.

Chapter Four

Clay assured himself that he only wanted to see Sarah again to show her the trunk. But when he opened the door to let her in, he knew he'd lied to himself.

The blue sky and the cheerful bird calls filling the air made for your average middle-of-May morning. But Sarah on the porch lifted the day from pleasant to near-perfect. She wasn't the most beautiful woman Clay had ever known, but at that moment, she ranked right up there.

Excitement radiated from her, making her eyes sparkle and tinting her cheeks pink. He wouldn't let himself even glance at her mouth, but his gaze unwittingly roved over the rest of her, to the bright blue blouse that curved over her small breasts, and lower, to the jeans that hugged her hips and long legs.

He cleared his throat. "You look rested." And hot. Very hot.

"I am. I slept really well."

She wouldn't have if she'd shared his bed. Images of her naked under him flitted through his head. Images that would only lead to trouble.

"Did you call your boyfriend and tell him about the footlocker?" he asked, wondering if she'd also mentioned that kiss.

"I'm not seeing anyone right now."

Clay half wished she was, if only to underline that she was off-limits.

"Are you going to let me in?" she asked, a smile tugging her lips.

Mentally smacking his head, he widened the door and stepped back. "I put the footlocker in the spare bedroom."

"The one where Tammy slept. Great."

She started forward, and Clay caught a whiff of that perfume.

And reminded himself that Sarah might smell and taste sweet, but underneath, she was anything but. She'd dissed him in print, and only a fool would forget that.

Best to let her take the trunk with her and sift through the contents someplace else. He opened his mouth to say so. "You want a cup of coffee?" came out instead. "It's leftover from breakfast," he added so she wouldn't think he'd made a pot special for her.

"That'd be great. I drink it black."

By the time he microwaved and brought the steaming mug to the spare bedroom, she was seated cross-legged on the braided rug in front of the open footlocker. She was holding on to Tammy's journal, running her fingertips slowly over the *Stay out!* warning, like a blind woman reading Braille.

She startled when she noticed him in the doorway, but also looked relieved that he'd come back. When she started to stand, Clay gestured at her to stay where she was and brought the mug to her.

"Thanks," she said with a fleeting smile.

Her fingers were ice-cold and her face pinched and anxious. Clay realized that, as eager as she was to learn about Tammy Becker, this was scary for her.

He hadn't intended to hang around, needed to contact the men who'd replied to his Craigslist ad and research new rodeo producers to contact. But Sarah looked up at him, her eyes wide and pleading for him to stay. Tethering him.

"This was Tammy's journal," she said in a voice that shook with feeling. "I've been so anxious to find out everything I can about her. But now…I don't know why I'm so hesitant to read it."

God help him, he couldn't leave her, not like this. "You want company?" he asked.

"I'm sure you have other things to do."

"Nothing that won't keep a few hours." He grabbed the flimsy chair from behind the student's desk. Straddling it backward, he sat down.

Sarah shot him a grateful look that made him feel good about staying, and opened the journal. "She started writing in here in January, 1982, on her fifteenth birthday. Listen to this. 'Marsha gave me this diary for my birthday. Rad! Mom and Dad said no boys could come to my party. They are so lame! The party was fun anyway. Marsha, Steffie and Jillian came. They're super lucky because they all have boyfriends. I don't, but I want one. When I get one, I'll have to sneak around. Mom and Dad don't want me doing anything except go to school, do my homework and go to church. Boooring.'"

Sarah glanced at Clay and shrugged. "That's it for the first journal entry." She thumbed through the pages. "She didn't write much in here." The pages rustled as she flipped to the end. "About a year later, she stopped altogether."

For a moment she was quiet, reading. "Listen to this, Clay. It's one of the last entries. 'My period was supposed to start two weeks ago. I've been a few days late before, but never this late. What if I'm pregnant? I can't be, or Mom and Dad will kill me.'"

Sarah bit her bottom lip. "She must've been so scared and lonely. Here's what she says a week later. 'Our youth group took a field trip to Regina, Canada. The bus ride took almost eight hours! Mrs. Guthrie made the boys and girls sit separately. She's almost as strict as my parents.

'After dinner, B and I snuck away from the other kids. We bought a pregnancy-test kit. You can get them in the drugstore up here—wait till I tell my friends. I couldn't take the test in my room, because I'm sharing with Misty Jones. If I spent too much time in the bathroom, she'd wonder what I was up to and tell on me. She's such a goody two shoes.

'So I took the test in the bathroom of a gas station while B waited for me outside the door.'" Sarah took a sip of her coffee. "I wonder who B is?"

"Probably the guy she was sleeping with."

"You mean my biological father. I'd sure like to know his name." She returned to the journal entry. "'The worst has happened. I'm pregnant. The whole rest of the trip and all the way home, I prayed and prayed to God to take this baby up to heaven. If He doesn't, B and I don't know what we'll do.' That's the last thing she wrote."

With a heavy sigh, Sarah closed the book. "Poor Tammy."

Clay was more interested in Sarah. Compassion and caring brushed her features with softness. Her eyes were shadowed and sorrowful, as if she knew exactly how Tammy had felt. For all Clay knew, she could've experienced a teenage pregnancy herself.

"Do you know anyone else who's gone through something like that?" he asked.

"A girl in my college dorm. But she was almost twenty-one. She and her boyfriend got married and as far as I know, they're happy. When you're sixteen, pregnancy has to be that much more difficult and lonely."

Clay knew something about teen pregnancy. "It is. My junior year of high school, one of my female friends got pregnant."

Sarah's expression shifted to surprise, then something much different. "Was the baby yours?"

The cool lift of her chin rankled. Figured she'd think that. "She was just a friend, Sarah. We never even kissed each other. My dad didn't want me getting into trouble like him. He raised me to be careful, and I always have been."

"With all the women you've slept with, you'd be crazy not to."

She sounded offended, almost angry. But her article had ruined his life, not the other way around. Clay bristled. "What have you got against me?"

"Nothing." Her lips clamped shut, but only for a moment. "What did your friend do about the baby?"

"Like the girl you knew in college, she got married. Because she and her boyfriend were so young, their parents had to sign a document that it was okay. But the marriage didn't work out, and a few months after their son was born, they split up. The baby's father paid what he could to help out, but he didn't have a high-school diploma, and didn't earn much. My friend ended up moving back in with her parents while she earned her GED and got on her feet financially."

Sarah looked thoughtful. "Do you think…do you think Tammy's parents accepted her pregnancy?"

"If they had, would she have given you up for adoption?"

"I don't know. Maybe." She hugged the journal close, the yearning on her face making Clay's chest ache. "I would guess that the family left town because of Tammy's pregnancy, except my birth certificate says I was born in Saddlers Prairie. But if they stayed here, why did they sell the house, and why did they leave this trunk and Tammy's bedroom furniture here? If this stuff is even hers."

She set the journal aside and massaged her temples, as if so many unknowns gave her a headache.

Clay could only wonder at the answers to those questions. Despite himself, he was beyond curious. He wanted to know what had happened to the Becker family, and especially Tammy. "She mentioned church a couple times, and her youth group. Maybe you can find out which one the family belonged to, and do some research there."

"Good idea. There can't be that many churches around here." Sarah gestured at the papers in the footlocker. "Maybe there's something in here about where the family went."

She rolled onto her knees in an easy move Clay envied. If he tried that, his bad knee would scream. Kneeling in front of the footlocker, she began to pull things out and stack them around her.

From where Clay sat, he had a great view of her backside. From time to time, her blouse rode up, revealing tantalizing glimpses of smooth skin. He told himself to look away, but didn't.

In no time, record albums, three-ring binders, spiral notebooks and a couple of skinny high-school yearbooks piled up around her. One too-tall stack toppled sideways, just missing Sarah's barely tasted coffee. Which was probably cold by now.

"Why don't you give me that mug," he said.

"Oh. Sure—thanks."

She arched backward and massaged the small of her back, causing her breasts to jut out. Clasping the handle of the mug, she reached across the mess, and handed it over. Her skin was warm now.

Clay was hot enough to boil water, and the brief slide of the backs of her fingers against his palm only upped his temperature.

Oblivious to his feelings, Sarah pored over an old report card. "This is from January of her junior year. I was born that August, which means she was barely pregnant. She may not even have known yet. She got an A in English, but almost flunked math. I was the same way." Sarah glanced around and frowned. "I don't see any other report cards. I wonder if they got tossed out, or maybe she dropped out of school before the end of her junior year."

"Could be either one. Why don't you check those yearbooks and see what you can find out? I'd start with the one from her junior year."

"There isn't one," she said. "Just the freshman and sophomore years. She went to a school called Four City High School."

"Saddlers Prairie is too small for its own high school," Clay told her. "We have a one-room school that goes through eighth grade. The older kids are bussed to the high school. If it were me, I'd check out Four City. Maybe one of her high-school teachers is still teaching there or lives somewhere close."

"I will." Sarah opened the yearbook from Tammy's sophomore year and propped the book on her lap. "Lots of kids signed Tammy's yearbook, but I don't see anything special. Just the usual, 'Have a great summer' and 'See you at church camp.' No mention of anyone with the initial B, and nothing signed by a boy whose name begins with that letter. But then, maybe Tammy didn't have a boyfriend yet. I wish she'd written something in her journal about him."

She flipped to the class pictures. After staring at the page with Tammy's photo, she held it up for Clay to see. "That's her, on the left. Neither of my adoptive parents had a wide mouth like mine, and I always wondered where I got it." Clearly emotional, she swallowed. "Now I know."

"Let me see that."

Clay stood. Sitting too long had caused his knee to stiffen up, and he winced as he joined Sarah on the rug.

"Are you in pain?"

"Still healing from an injury." Not wanting to invite questions, which would lead to the pity he detested, he studied the yearbook.

The girl staring from the photo was pretty, with big eyes and a begging-to-be-kissed bottom lip, a teenage version of Sarah. "You have her face shape and eyes, too," he said.

"I noticed that." She fiddled with an earring. "I wonder what color her eyes were. With black-and-white photos, you can't tell."

Clay had no idea and didn't care. He was lost in the expressive depths of Sarah's eyes. Something sweet and warm passed between them, a bond of sorts, born out of sharing the contents of the old footlocker.

Cheeks flushed, she dropped her gaze to the yearbook on her lap. "I wish there were more pictures of her. And at least one of her parents. My grandparents."

Though her gaze remained on the yearbook, Clay had the feeling she wasn't seeing it.

"I hardly remember my adoptive grandparents," she said. "A car accident took my maternal grandparents before I was born, and I was three when my father's parents died in a plane crash. Two horrible tragedies."

Clay had always taken his parents and four grandparents for granted. They all lived a few miles from each other in Billings, along with his aunt, his sister, her husband and their two kids. He'd never even imagined what his life would've been like without them.

Sarah had no living relatives except, possibly, for her biological parents and grandparents—people she'd never even met. That had to feel lonely, worse than any emptiness Clay had experienced.

"You never know, you might find photos buried somewhere in this stuff," he said.

"Which is why I'm going to look carefully through everything."

That could take hours—days, for that matter. He didn't think he'd be able to handle having Sarah around that long.

Looking thoughtful, she tapped her finger to her mouth. "I wonder what her friends thought about the pregnancy, and how the school reacted."

"Thirty years ago, in a small town? Probably not well."

Once more, her beautiful eyes met his. "I feel so bad for Tammy. I would really like to meet her and talk about it."

Clay hoped she got that chance. He wanted her to find and reunite with her relatives, so that the shadows and worry faded from her face.

"You don't have to worry about me, Clay," she said

as if she'd read his mind. "I've been alone for a while now, and I'm okay."

He had no doubt of that. He'd never met a woman like her. She was strong and didn't flirt or fall all over him.

Most of the women he'd known said what they thought he wanted to hear, instead of speaking their minds. Sarah didn't seem to have that problem. At times, she seemed cool and distant, but right now, she was open and warm, just as when she'd followed him around for that piece she was writing about him.

Back then, he'd been so sure she cared for him—not as a rodeo star, as a man.

Her behavior after that kiss had proved the opposite.

He'd liked her three years ago, and fool that he was, he liked her now. Whether she cared for him any more than she had then was anyone's guess, and if he knew what was good for him, he'd get rid of her now.

He rolled his tense shoulders and cleared his throat. "I need to make a few calls and tackle some chores."

"Of course." Sarah glanced at her watch. "I've been here two whole hours? I had no idea this would take so much time, and I've barely touched the surface. There's still tons of stuff to go through. Would you mind if I took the footlocker back to Mrs. Yancy's?"

Clay didn't care what she took, so long as she left. "It doesn't belong to me or Ty, so I don't see why not." Ignoring his protesting leg, he pushed to his feet with barely a wince. "So you're staying with Mrs. Yancy?"

"That's right." She began to pile things back into the trunk. "Do you know her?"

"We've met. She talks a lot."

Sarah grinned at that. "Yes, she does." Having returned everything to the footlocker, she closed the lid and fastened it. He offered her a hand up.

Much too late and all too soon, she pulled free.

"She means well, though," she said. "I think she's lonely. She's a great cook. This morning, she made the best breakfast."

"That'd compensate for a lot of chatter."

Sarah laughed, and for that moment her cares seemed to fall away. Her wide, perfect smile took his breath away.

It was all Clay could do to not pull her close and move in for another sizzling kiss. He backed toward the door.

"Right, you have things to do," she said, misinterpreting his retreat. "Thanks for sitting with me while I looked through this stuff. Having you here made the whole process easier for me."

But not for him. Since yesterday's kiss, his body had awakened after a long drought, and a certain part of him was raring to go. He gave a grudging nod, and then hefted the footlocker to his shoulder.

It wasn't that heavy, but Sarah's eyes widened, and he thought he saw admiration on her face. She grabbed her purse and collected her mug from the floor. "I'll drop this off in the kitchen."

Clay nodded and followed her from the room. She moved fast, her hips swinging. She wasn't trying to be provocative. All the same, she was.

He felt bewitched. Gobsmacked. In lust.

By the time Sarah returned from the kitchen and joined him at the door, he was fighting a hard-on. Lucky for him, her attention was on the load balanced on his shoulder.

She opened the screen door for him, holding it while he maneuvered through with the footlocker. His forearm accidentally brushed her soft breasts. A jolt of pure, hot desire surged through him, and he nearly dropped the trunk.

Sarah blushed.

"Uh, sorry about that," he lied.

He moved past her, when what he really wanted was to get a whole lot closer.

Outside, she fell into step beside him. Too close, and Clay gripped the footlocker and lengthened his stride. His leg protested, but the pain was a small price to pay for putting more space between them.

Dimly, he registered that for the first time this spring, the air was hot. He forced himself to pay attention to the penned dogs in his neighbor's yard, barking out hellos, and noted that one of the flowering bushes had burst into bloom. Anything to distract him from the woman a few feet behind him.

None of it made a whit of difference. Blood pounded in his head, and his long-denied body homed in on her and refused to leave things be. He figured he'd cool down once she drove off.

Standing back, he waited for her to pop the trunk of her car. He set the footlocker in, slammed the lid shut and then made a show of checking his watch.

Sarah started for the driver's side of the car, but stopped and turned toward him. "I almost forgot—Mrs. Yancy told me about your ranch."

"It won't be up and running for a while yet," he said in a gruff voice.

"That's a huge change from rodeoing."

A tiny bit of paper was stuck in her hair. To stop himself from reaching out and removing it, which would be dangerous, he shoved his hands in the rear pockets of his jeans. "My life is totally different now. A lot quieter. Buckle bunnies don't flock around me, and reporters don't call."

Why had he told her?

"Do you miss the attention?"

"Not really. I've been too busy, focusing on the ranch. It needed a ton of work." Repairing the dilapidated outbuildings and researching the stock-contracting business had taken a huge chunk of time, effort and money. "I don't have any cattle yet, and I haven't hired a crew, but I'm working on both." After the crew was in place and settled into their trailers, he would put them to work, repairing and replacing fencing so that he could safely pen his stock. It was work he'd attempted to tackle himself, but his bum leg made for slow, painful progress.

"I'm sure you'll do very well."

She looked and sounded as if she believed in him. These days, not a lot of people did. That felt good, made him want to show her his property and share the house plans.

"I'd like to interview you about what's involved in setting up a ranch," she said.

"For the article you're writing?" he guessed.

She nodded. Clay didn't trust her enough.

He didn't trust himself, either.

He rocked back on his heels. "I don't think so."

"I guess I'm not surprised." She looked half-sorry for the lies she'd written, and for a moment he thought she might apologize.

Instead she blew out a breath and shook her head in disbelief. "The article came out almost three years ago, Clay. I don't understand why you're still so angry."

Because his life had been forever changed. "You left a day early, without so much as a goodbye, and you never answered my calls or emails," he said. "Never even gave me the courtesy of an explanation, just left me to deal with the fallout. Why'd you do it, Sarah? Why did you tell those lies about me?"

Chapter Five

Sarah had seen Clay laugh, had seen him serious, somber and irritated, but until now, she'd never seen him truly angry. The sheer size of the man, combined with the ominous gleam in his narrowed eyes was intimidating and then some.

Briefly, she considered jumping into her car, locking all the doors and speeding away, but she was upset with him, too. This was the second time he'd called her a liar. She wasn't. She took her writing career far too seriously to fabricate anything,

Once and for all, it was time to set Clay straight.

Trembling inside—whether from fear, anger or a combination of both—she squared her shoulders and raised her chin. "I left early because I had all the information I needed and there was no reason to stay. And as I explained before, every word of that article was the God's honest truth."

Clay snorted. "Let me refresh your memory. And I quote, 'Clay Hollyer is as talented a bull rider as you'll ever meet, with an ego as big as the crossbred Brahma bulls he so skillfully stays astride. To see him in his chaps, denim shirt and Stetson, holding tight to the bull rope while his powerful legs grip the bucking bull is to witness the unforgettable spectacle of man against eighteen hundred pounds of turbo-charged animal.

"'A ten-time world champion, and as friendly as he is talented, the popular Hollyer is often sought out by fans for photos. Women travel from around the country to seek out the wealthy, handsome bachelor, in hopes of lassoing his heart. He has been linked with numerous females, including models and actresses. But never for long. Buckle bunnies, the groupies of the rodeo world, vie and flirt for his attention like bees around honey.'"

Sarah opened her mouth, but Clay wasn't finished.

"'Clay is the number-one bull rider in the country and a skilled lover,' enthused one buckle bunny who wishes to remain anonymous,'" he went on. "'I'd be crazy to not want a few hours alone with him.'"

He shut his mouth, rested his hands low on his narrow hips, no sign of the Hollyer charm in sight.

"You memorized all that?" She managed a smile at odds with her trembling insides. "I'm flattered and impressed."

She was also taken aback. She'd never heard the words spoken out loud, and that part of the five-thousand-word article sounded more tabloidlike than she'd intended.

"Every word is burned into my mind. You all but came out and called me shallow, vain and sex-obsessed."

"Well, aren't you?" she countered, though after this morning, he no longer seemed either shallow or vain. "Most men would appreciate being praised for their skills in the bedroom."

"That's not what I object to. I'm a red-blooded guy. Of course I like sex. You're a healthy, beautiful woman, and I'll bet my truck that you enjoy it, too." He raised an eyebrow, daring her to argue.

He thought she was beautiful, which surprised her. He was also right—she did like sex and thought about it a lot, probably because she hadn't been with anyone since Matthew.

"I don't want anything serious, and I've always been up front about that," he went on. "I don't have to explain myself to you or anyone else."

She wasn't about to point out that he'd just spent several minutes doing just that. She was on the verge of asking what he specifically objected to, when he told her.

"That so-called quote from the buckle bunny just about ruined my life. How would you like to come home from an exhausting road trip to find a couple of women camped at your door, waiting to join you in bed? Trust me, it's not half as fun as it sounds."

The thought of Clay in bed with two buckle bunnies at the same time did not sit well, and only proved Sarah's point. "The quote was real," she said. "The bunny you slept with a couple of nights before I left was only too happy to sing your sexual praises. I'll bet you don't even remember her name. Well, don't ask me, because I refuse to divulge my source."

"So that's what all that stuff was about—some groupie I spent an hour with." Clay snorted. "Your article ruined my life. You're lucky I didn't sue your cute little ass."

"Ruined your life? That's quite an exaggeration."

"Nope. One of the many women who read your article and showed up at my door later claimed that I impregnated her. I was pretty sure I hadn't because like I said, I always use protection. She was lying, of course— a DNA test proved that."

Sarah hadn't realized. "That's terrible, Clay, but I'm

not responsible for the woman's behavior, and I doubt that your life was ruined because of it."

"You have no idea."

None at all, and she wanted to know. "What hap—"

"I don't want to talk about it." He compressed his lips.

"All right, but since we're airing complaints, here's mine. When we met nearly three years ago, you led me on." He'd treated her as if she was special to him. That was before she'd overheard the two buckle bunnies and realized she wasn't. "I actually thought you liked me. You kissed me that way."

"I did like you."

"And yet, the night before, you had sex with some bunny. I don't understand how you can have sex with one person and the very next day, kiss someone else as if she mattered."

"What I did with her had nothing to do with you and me. Besides, I had no idea I was ever going to kiss you, not until just before I did it." His gaze dropped to her mouth. "You're right about one thing, though. That kiss meant something."

His eyelids dropped a fraction over his very warm gaze, seductive and intent. Making her feel restless and needy. She half wished he'd kiss her again.

She posed the question that had plagued her ever since. "Why *did* you kiss me, Clay?"

"Because that mouth… I thought… We both…" He broke off and blew out a loud breath. "To hell with the past, Sarah."

With a dangerous glint in his eyes, he started toward her. Unable to move, she swallowed. "What are you doing?"

"What I've wanted to do since you knocked on my

door this morning." He cupped her face between his big rough hands, and brushed her bangs back with his fingers.

"Please, Clay," she whispered, not sure whether she wanted him to let go of her or step closer.

The corner of his mouth lifted. Angling his head, he kissed her.

SARAH TOLD HERSELF to pull away, but she wanted this. Clay's mouth, eager and hungry on hers, his muscular arms tight around her.

She was barely aware that she was walking backward, his thighs prodding her legs to move, until she bumped against the car.

He caught hold of her hands and pinned them against his solid chest. Right over his thudding heart.

Which was beating as hard as hers.

Nudging his leg between hers, he kissed her again. Several times. Long, deep, tongue kisses that stole her breath and obliterated her common sense.

Not hiding what she wanted, she slid her hands up his chest, twined her arms around his neck and kissed him back with the same hunger.

Clay groaned and thrust his tongue against hers in a tangle of slickness and heat. His restless hands explored her back and wandered lower. He palmed her behind and anchored her against his groin.

He was aroused.

Dampness flooded her panties and her breasts swelled and tightened. "Clay," she pleaded, breathless.

"What?" he murmured, before taking her in another searing kiss.

Moaning, she hooked her foot around his calf. "Touch me."

He slid his hand under her blouse, up her stomach and toward her breasts. As she inched back to give him access, a car honked.

"You go, bull rider!" a man yelled.

Sarah and Clay jerked apart.

Muttering, he scrubbed his hand over his face. "Great, just great, something for the gossip mill. I'll never live this down."

Sarah was sure he would. And she was thankful people around here didn't know who she was. Whoever had called out probably figured she was some buckle bunny. Clay said they didn't come around anymore, but Sarah guessed that from time to time, a woman or two knocked at his door.

How many others had he kissed—and more—since he'd moved to Saddlers Prairie? Sarah didn't want to be one of the many.

Feeling foolish and mad at herself for falling into his arms and responding to his attention, even if he was the best kisser she'd ever known, she straightened her top. "Goodbye, Clay, and thanks for the footlocker."

She felt his eyes on her as she pulled the car door closed and started the engine, but she wouldn't let herself look at him.

Confused and disappointed at her weakness for this cowboy, a man who would never return the feelings she admitted she still carried for him, she drove back to Mrs. Yancy's.

AROUND LUNCHTIME FRIDAY afternoon, Clay arrived at his ranch to interview a man for the foreman job, the first of the crew he needed to hire.

He was nearly an hour early, giving him time to check in with Garrett McReedy, his builder. Clay headed toward the giant hole where the former wreck of a house had stood.

After tearing down and carting away the debris from it and enlarging the hole to accommodate a bigger structure, the construction workers had poured the foundation. At last.

Building a custom house took time, and progress was slow. Too slow for Clay, who wanted to move to the ranch as soon as possible. He half wished he'd moved into one of the trailers on the ranch, but they were for his future crew.

McReedy assured him that his men were on schedule to finish around Thanksgiving.

The all-male construction crew sat eating lunch among piles of building supplies. Every one of them called out a greeting. A gangly male who looked all of eighteen stood and shyly approached Clay.

"I'm a real fan," he said, extending his hand. "I'm honored for the privilege of building your house, and I promise to give this job my very best."

Clay nodded. "I appreciate that."

"Would you mind if one of the guys snapped a photo of us together?"

Clay fielded the same question several times a week. Even when he'd been at the top of his game, he'd never enjoyed posing with strangers. Now that his bull-riding days were over and he was a has-been—the ex-bull rider with the bum leg everyone felt sorry for—he detested the practice.

But the kid looked so eager that Clay couldn't turn him down. He shrugged. "Why not."

One of the men snapped several photos with his phone, and the kid beamed.

"Thanks, Clay. This is sure to earn me big points with my girlfriend."

Whatever floated her boat. "Where's your boss?" Clay asked.

"In the trailer."

Clay crossed the hard ground, stirring up dust despite Wednesday's rainstorm. The earth begged for a grassy yard. All in good time.

He knocked on the trailer door before poking his head inside.

Garrett McReedy sat as his desk, munching a sandwich, studying the blueprints and tapping at his laptop.

"Hey," Clay said, entering the room. "You wanted to show me the custom windows?"

The builder nodded in greeting. "I don't want to order them without your okay. They're gonna be real pretty, and the triple insulation will cut down on your heating and cooling bills." Clay sat down across the desk, and Garrett turned the laptop toward him. "Take a look at this picture-window mock-up for the great room and see what you think."

While Garrett explained how the window was constructed, Clay studied the drawing. "I like it."

"At the price these babies cost, you'd better. Here are a couple more. These will face south."

They continued this way, Garrett showing Clay various windows and asking questions. While Garrett scribbled notes and tapped at his laptop, Clay thought about Sarah.

Part of him wanted to show her the house plans so she'd know that despite his fall from celebrity, his bank account was healthy. Another part of him knew better.

He'd thought a lot about yesterday. About her. Her elation over the footlocker and her bad case of nerves.

The gratitude she'd shown when he stuck around and kept her company.

She'd been so mad and defensive when he'd called her out for the things she'd written about him. He hadn't exactly been cool and calm, either. Yet despite his anger, the defiant spark in her eyes had turned him on. But then everything about her did.

He hadn't wanted a woman this way for a long time, and holding and kissing her again had felt good. Really, really good.

But kisses weren't nearly enough—for either of them.

Sarah's response to him proved that she wanted him, too. The two of them together were like a brush fire about to grow into raging flames. Which was dangerous on so many levels.

If he were smart, he'd back away from her. Unfortunately, he wasn't. Having been around this block many times, Clay knew exactly what his strong feelings meant. He was infatuated with Sarah, and sooner or later, his desire, his lust, would fade away.

She was only in town two weeks, not long enough to get too involved. The perfect scenario—if she were anyone else. But Sarah was special and he didn't want to hurt her. Or to get hurt himself. He didn't trust her.

For those reasons, it was better for them both if he pulled back while he still could. No matter how badly he wanted her.

"I wish I'd thought to build a house as big as this one when I was your age," Garrett said. "You're smart to think ahead for when you get married and have kids."

"I don't see that happening."

"With all the beautiful woman in your life, I understand." Garrett shook his head. "Me, I'm happy with

Charlotte." He glanced at the framed color photo of him and his wife that hung on the wall.

A goofy, still-on-our-honeymoon smile lit his face, but they'd recently celebrated their seven-year anniversary. His wife was pregnant now, due about the time Clay's house would be finished. "You sure you want four bedrooms and three-and-a-half baths?"

Clay nodded. "I have a big family, and I want room for when they come visit."

"Works for me." Garrett's watch beeped. He crumpled his sandwich wrapper. "Back to the salt mines. What's on your agenda this afternoon?"

"I'm meeting a potential foreman here."

"Good luck with that. If anything else comes up with the house, I'll call you."

"Thanks, man."

They shook hands and exited the trailer. As the construction crew donned hard hats and started back to work, a battered red truck drove up and parked beside Clay's.

A forty-something, bowlegged cowboy built like a linebacker gone to seed slid from the driver's seat and approached Clay.

"Mr. Hollyer? I'm Stanley Mattson, but I go by Burl."

With his barrel chest, the nickname made sense. Clay nodded. "You can call me Clay."

Burl's grip was strong and his gaze direct. Despite his less-than-fit appearance, after a few minutes of talking, Clay knew he could do the job. His resume showed that over the past twenty-five years he'd worked at just two ranches, and he had experience with every ranching chore imaginable.

Machinery pounded loudly at the construction site, making conversation difficult.

"Let's walk and talk," Clay said over the noise. "I'll show you around."

"I expect you want to know why I moved ranches," Burl said as they headed toward the barn. "The first time, the family sold to a corporation that laid us all off. I'd been there ten years, since I was eighteen. Then I was hired as foreman at the ranch I'm with now. Figured I'd be there forever, but times being hard and all, they're about to go belly-up. The boss just laid me off, along with the rest of the crew."

"That's tough," Clay said.

Mattson shrugged. "Sometimes a man's gotta roll with the punches, pick himself up off the ground and start over again."

If that didn't describe the past year of Clay's life to a T. With that, he made up his mind. "If you want the job, you can move into the foreman's cottage this weekend and start work Monday. There's plenty of fencing to be done, and an auction next Wednesday. You can come with me and help me choose the right stock."

They discussed money and job duties, and shook hands. Clay showed him the cottage and gave him a key. "Tell those crew members who worked for you to get in touch if they want a job here," he said.

"Will do."

Mattson drove off.

One huge item checked off Clay's to-do list. A weight fell off his shoulders. There was plenty more to do before the ranch was up and running, but he was off to a decent start.

Chapter Six

Saturday morning, Sarah stood at the open closet door in her rented room and eyed the clothes she'd brought. She wanted to look professional, yet not overly dressed up.

Lucky Arnett, the rancher she was about to interview, probably didn't expect her to wear a skirt and pantyhose, but she wasn't about to show up in faded jeans and a T-shirt, either. She decided on cowboy boots, navy jeans, a crisp blouse and a blazer.

She'd wasted yesterday afternoon driving twenty miles to Four City High School, where she'd attempted to get the names and contact information for teachers and administrators who'd worked at the school when Tammy had attended. Pre-internet, of course. Sarah had learned that the school had burned down ten years ago, and all files had been lost. She had also spoken with the secretary at the one church in town, a woman unfamiliar with the Becker family. She'd left messages at other churches within a ten-mile radius of Saddlers Prairie, but as of yet, nothing had come of that, or of a closer look at Tammy's things.

If only she'd recorded her thoughts and feelings about the pregnancy. If only she'd named the father.

It was all so frustrating, and after so much fruitless

work Sarah looked forward to focusing on the upcoming interview and forgetting about Tammy Becker for a while.

Standing in front of the vanity mirror over the dresser, she applied gloss to her parted lips. Lips Clay had looked at with such desire that she'd melted even before he'd kissed her. Remembering, her lips tingled and her nipples tightened.

"What do you expect after more than a year of celibacy?" she asked herself, frowning.

But did the man she wanted have to be Clay Hollyer?

"No more kissing Clay," she sternly added. Since she doubted she'd see him again, that shouldn't be a problem.

Suddenly, Mrs. Yancy called out from the bottom of the stairs. "Sarah? Would you like something to eat before you leave?"

Sarah didn't want to put the woman out, especially when she was supposed to take care of lunch on her own. "I'll grab something on the way," she called back. "But thanks. I'll be right there."

She loaded her notebook, tape recorder and camera into her equipment bag and headed downstairs.

Mrs. Yancy was waiting for her in the living room. "I packed you a lunch anyway," she said, handing Sarah a brown paper bag. "Now don't fret, it isn't much— just a sandwich, an apple and a couple of double-chocolate-drop cookies." She nodded at a foil-covered plate. "Those are for Lucky. He likes sweets and doesn't have anyone cooking for him, and I know he'll appreciate them."

"I'm sure he will." Having talked briefly with Mr. Arnett on the phone, Sarah knew he was an older man.

Maybe Mrs. Yancy was interested in him. "Is he a widower?" she asked, studying the older woman closely.

"Lucky? Heavens, no. He never married. He's in his seventies now, and was a customer of John's from way back. Over the years, they became friends and used to fish together. Now and then, after a long day at the river, John would bring him home to supper. That's how I learned about his sweet tooth. My John had one, too. Those two could eat a whole pie in one sitting and never gain an ounce. That used to make me so mad."

Mrs. Yancy shook her head and smiled, as if reliving pleasant memories.

Sarah wondered if she'd ever have memories of a husband, and a son or daughter to share them with. Someday, she assured herself. She wasn't even thirty yet, and still had time to have babies. All she needed was to meet the right man.

"These days, Lucky and I hardly see each other," Mrs. Yancy went on, "but I always bring him cookies on his birthday and over the holidays."

Sarah marveled at the woman's thoughtfulness. She seemed to have a big heart and a generous spirit. So different from Ellen, who always kept score of who she gave gifts to, whether or not they returned the favor and whether the value of their gift matched hers.

Sarah had never understood that side of Ellen, and vaguely remembered that things had seemed different when her adoptive father was alive. She had a few hazy memories of family vacations that included impulsive presents for friends, laughter and warm hugs.

"Be sure to ask Lucky about the time the plague of locusts swarmed through his alfalfa crop," Mrs. Yancy said. "It's quite a story."

Sarah nodded. "I have no idea what time I'll be back."

"No worries. I'm going to a Saturday-night movie party, where we watch a DVD over dinner. After the movie, we discuss it, and when the girls and I get to talking, we tend to run late. Don't wait up for me."

LUCKY ARNETT'S RANCH was all the way across town, a good fifteen-mile drive from Mrs. Yancy's. The day was warm, and Sarah opened the sunroof and cranked up the music.

Signs of spring were everywhere, from the bright flowers dotting the long prairie grass on either side of the highway, to the aroma of sweet clover and other plants she couldn't identify, and the baby calves trailing their mothers in distant pastures.

On the drive, she passed several fenced pastures and outbuildings that undoubtedly belonged to various ranches. None were identified in any way that she could see, and she couldn't help wondering if one of the ranches belonged to Clay.

She wanted to see his ranch, wanted to know more about the business he was starting. Too bad he'd turned down the offer of an interview.

Sarah couldn't really blame him, and wished now that she'd tempered some of what she'd written for the magazine. Not that she felt in any way responsible for the woman who Clay claimed had ruined his life. Still, she *had* been angry and hurt when she'd written the article, which was hardly professional, and in hindsight, a total overreaction. She'd had no claim on Clay. After all, they'd never discussed starting a relationship or even dating, and he'd only kissed her once.

But that kiss had felt like a promise.

Sarah was no innocent. She'd kissed lots of men, and had had her share of lovers. But Clay brought kissing to a whole new level, his lips eager and warm and giving. With a whole lot of heart, just as she'd always imagined a man interested in the long-term would.

Unfortunately, Clay just happened to kiss that way, which was where the trouble had started.

Knowing that did nothing to dampen her reaction to him now. His kisses weren't all that drew her. She thought about the footlocker and her reluctance to look through Tammy's things by herself. Clay had given up several hours of his time to keep her company. There weren't a lot of guys who'd do that.

He was different than she'd ever guessed and in many ways a good man. With a weakness for women, she reminded herself. Sometimes two at the same time.

That was one reason getting involved with him was a bad idea.

Ahead, she saw the Lucky A Ranch sign, hanging prominently from an iron arch spanning a winding gravel driveway. Sarah signaled and drove under the sign, which needed a paint touch-up. About fifty feet ahead sat a weathered house with a wraparound porch. There were other aging buildings nearby, some in better shape than others.

Yet despite the less-than-optimal condition of the buildings, the lush fields, herds of lowing cattle and men hard at work showed that this ranch was alive and kicking.

Sarah slung her equipment bag over her shoulder and exited the car. From behind the house, an older man approached. Tall and wiry, his gray hair cut military short, he clasped a cigarette between thin lips.

"You must be Mr. Arnett," she said, offering her hand. "I'm Sarah Tigarden."

"Folks call me Lucky." With a somber expression the rancher briefly clasped her hand in a firm, callused grip.

"I have something for you." She retrieved the plate of cookies from the passenger seat of the car. "These are from Mrs. Yancy."

At last, Lucky smiled, his sharp blue eyes crinkling at the corners. "Paula never forgets me, and for that, I'm one grateful cowboy." He tossed the butt into the dirt and ground it out with the toe of his boot, then peeled back the foil and helped himself. "Double-chocolate-drop cookies—my favorites. You want one?"

Having eaten her own cookies on the drive over, Sarah shook her head.

"I'll set these inside," Lucky said, chewing. "Then I'll show you around."

He didn't invite her in. While she waited, she dug into her bag for the camera and snapped pictures of the barn, house and the vast fields beyond.

Up close, the buildings were even shabbier than she'd first thought. Especially the barn. The roof had been patched in several places, and here and there new siding, primed but as yet unpainted, replaced various sections of wall.

Lucky stepped onto the porch with a thermos and two plastic cups. "How about coffee?"

Sarah had already enjoyed several delicious cups of Mrs. Yancy's brew and didn't need more, but she wasn't about to turn down Lucky's hospitality.

She nodded, and he set both cups on the porch railing and filled them. After a long pull from his cup, Lucky smacked his lips. "Now that's what I call high-octane."

Sarah liked her coffee strong, but this stuff was turbocharged, bitter and so thick she could've spooned it into her mouth. She couldn't hide her grimace.

Lucky chuckled, as if pleased by her reaction. "Don't worry, it only *tastes* like it'll put hair on your chest. Come on, I'll show you around."

When he wasn't looking, she tossed the remains into the bushes, silently apologizing to the poor plants.

"My granddad started this ranch," Lucky explained as they ambled toward the barn. "His specialty was cattle, but he also dabbled in alfalfa. He managed all right, but he borrowed on the land, and when he passed my daddy inherited a mountain of debt along with the ranch.

"He and mama scrabbled to hold on to the property. Now it's mine. I haven't been able to make it hum the way I dreamed, but I'm getting along well enough."

It was obvious that he loved the ranch. "What will happen to it when you…" Not sure how to phrase the rest of the question delicately, Sarah broke off.

"When I pass? It'll go to my niece, Gina, but she doesn't know it yet. She lives in Chicago."

Chicago and Saddlers Prairie were worlds apart. "Does she like ranching?" Sarah ventured.

"She did when she was little. She lived here in town until she graduated high school. She put herself through college and has a degree in marketing. Gina's a smart one, and I'm betting on her. This here's the barn."

The big doors creaked loudly as he pushed them open.

Sarah stepped into a barn straight out of a fairy tale: big, lofty and airy, smelling of hay, horses and leather. Shelves and wall hooks contained horse gear and farming tools.

"This is really nice," she said.

Lucky gave her a sideways look, clearly doubting her sincerity.

"I mean it," she said. "I've never been in a barn before, and yours is exactly what I imagine it should be."

The rancher seemed satisfied with this, and almost smiled.

"Do you mind if I ask a few questions and record your answers?" she asked.

"Not at all. Fire away."

Lucky patiently answered every question she asked with painful honesty. He didn't hide the hardships he endured, including the time when the locusts had stripped his fields bare, and allowed her to snap photos.

As they headed for one of the cattle pastures to see some of the herd up close, a big man about Sarah's age strode toward them.

"That there's my right-hand man," Lucky said. "Come on, and I'll introduce you."

He lengthened his stride and whipped forward. Sarah scrambled to keep up.

"This is Zach Horton, my foreman," Lucky said. "The day I met him was the day I finally lived up to the name 'Lucky.' Zach knows plenty about ranching, so feel free to ask him anything. You want numbers to back up what I told you, Zach'll give them to you."

A look passed between the two men, and Zach nodded.

His direct gaze impressed Sarah. He was very good-looking and seemed friendly, but he wasn't nearly as magnetic as Clay.

Sarah frowned. She had to stop thinking about him.

"I'll leave you two to talk while I take care of a few things." Lucky turned to Sarah. "Don't leave without saying goodbye."

"I won't. Thanks for your time, Lucky. He was about to show me how to spot a pregnant cow," Sarah said as the old rancher strode off.

"All right. Follow me."

As Lucky had, Zach allowed Sarah to record him. The old rancher hadn't been kidding—his foreman knew his ranching and understood the numbers behind the business. Zach explained the costs involved in running the ranch and how food prices caused big fluctuations in profit margins. He didn't hide how the downward trend of beef prices had hurt not just the Lucky A, but all cattle ranches.

A busy man, he cut off the conversation all too soon. Sarah understood, but was sorry the interview had to end. There was so much yet to learn. Still, she'd gathered lots of useful information, and had no doubt that the Dawson brothers and the other ranchers on her list would add to her knowledge base.

"I appreciate your time, Zach," she said.

"No problem. If you want to say goodbye to Lucky, you'll find him in the tractor shed behind the house."

Sarah peeked inside what smelled like an auto-body garage. "I'm leaving now," she told the rancher. "Thanks for letting me spend a few hours with you and Zach. This has been really interesting and fun."

"Hold on and I'll walk you to your car." Lucky wiped his hands on his jeans. "I trust Zach answered all your questions?" he asked as they crossed the backyard.

"He was great. You both were. Thanks again for your time."

"Thanks for your interest in the Lucky A."

"I'll send you two copies of the article," she said at the car. "One for you and one for Zach."

"That'd be great. Who else are you planning to interview?"

"I'm scheduled to meet with Dawson brothers at their ranch on Monday."

Lucky nodded his approval. "They're good men who make a real comfortable living. Anyone else?"

"Mrs. Yancy mentioned a few. Who do you suggest?"

Lucky rubbed his chin. "There's a newcomer to town you might want to talk to, young fella by the name of Clay Hollyer. Used to be a bull rider, and could he ride.

"Couple years ago, he had a bad accident and crushed his knee to smithereens. Just thinking about it makes my own knees hurt. Clay can't ride anymore, so he's getting into the ranching business. But not in the traditional sense. He'll be dealing in stock for rodeos—bulls and steers."

Clay hadn't told Sarah the extent of his injury, which sounded excruciatingly painful and explained the limp.

"I'll keep him in mind," she said.

Keep him in mind? Between her own wayward feelings and the constant mention of his name, she was finding it virtually impossible to *not* think about him.

TIRED OF HIS own company, Clay stopped at a tavern just outside town on Saturday afternoon. Sparky's offered on-tap beer, lively music and decent food.

It was early yet, and the place was quiet, which suited him fine. He wasn't in the mood to deal with rodeo fans and pretend he was still a star.

As he looked around for a place to park his butt, he noticed a blonde with big breasts perched on one of the stools—just his type. Her lashes lowered, and she gave him a come-on-over look.

Last time that had happened, about six weeks before

Clay had moved to Saddlers Prairie some two months ago, he'd been learning to walk with a cane, and had gone without sex for over a year. A blonde not unlike the one across the room had slid onto the stool beside him and struck up a flirty conversation. He'd ended up buying them both a few drinks too many, getting wasted and going home with her.

Which had taken care of his physical needs, but had otherwise left him dissatisfied. When he sobered up some hours later, he left and never saw her again.

Maybe it was the accident, or maybe he was getting old, but from now on he wanted to get to know a woman before taking her to bed.

Between building his leg strength, getting the ranch in shape and working on the house plans, he hadn't even tried to get to know any females in Saddlers Prairie. Which was why, since that sorry night, he hadn't so much as kissed a woman.

Then Sarah had knocked at his door.

Clay hadn't seen her for two days and didn't want to think about her or those red-hot kisses. But his mind rebelled, and his body…he glanced down at himself and snickered.

The blonde was still smiling. Ignoring her, he stepped up to the opposite side of the bar.

The bartender, a forty-something guy with a receding hairline and handlebar moustache, came right over. "You're Clay Hollyer," he said, looking awed. "I heard that you moved to Saddlers Prairie. Welcome to Sparky's."

Clay managed a tight smile. "Thanks. What's on tap tonight?"

The bartender told him, and he ordered a beer, a double cheeseburger and fries.

"Word is, there's a woman in town writing a story about ranching and researching people by the name of Becker," the bartender said when he set a frosty mug in front of Clay. "I heard she stopped by your place the other day, looking for information."

"That's right," Clay said, not at all surprised. In a town the size of Saddlers Prairie, people knew things. He tilted his mug in salute and sipped.

The bartender left to help other customers before returning with Clay's meal. "I know a Mr. and Mrs. Becker."

About to bite into his burger, Clay paused. "Do they have a daughter named Tammy?"

"Beats me. I only met them once, when I visited my great aunt. She lives at Sunset Manor, and so do they."

"What's Sunset Manor?" he asked around a mouthful.

"A retirement home some twenty-five-odd miles from here. The writer lady could probably call and find out if they're the Beckers she's looking for."

Clay nodded. "Thanks for the tip. I'll pass it along."

What a great lead, and while he ate, he thought about Sarah. She was bound to be pleased, especially if the Beckers at Sunset Manor turned out to be her grandparents.

No doubt she'd also be nervous like she was about the footlocker. She'd probably chew on her soft lower lip like crazy....

His body rallied at the thought, and he almost groaned in frustration. A healthy swig of beer helped.

As soon as he went home, he'd call and tell her what the barkeep had shared. Then he'd leave her alone. She was safer that way, and so was he.

He just hoped things worked out for her.

Chapter Seven

After giving up her weekends—her *life*—for a year, Sarah made a point of going out often, especially on a Saturday night. In Boise, there were always plenty of options—movies, concerts, plays, dinner with friends, shopping and more.

But here in Saddlers Prairie, where she had no friends and there wasn't much in the way of entertainment, figuring out where to go and what to do for the evening wasn't so easy. The *Saddlers Prairie News,* the local monthly paper, wasn't much help, and an online search of things to do in the area yielded dismal results. Sarah wished she'd asked Mrs. Yancy for suggestions. But Mrs. Yancy was at the movie party with her friends.

Sarah was alone and on her own, and wasn't *that* the story of her life.

A wave of loneliness washed over her, and she seriously considered crawling into bed, pulling the covers over her head and sleeping away the blues. Then she caught herself and frowned. Hosting her own pity party was the last thing she needed.

Determined to get out and enjoy herself, she straightened her shoulders and thought about dinner. It was almost dinnertime. After several nights of pizza and fast food, she was ready for something better. Mrs. Yancy claimed that Barb's Café was good. Why not try it tonight?

While she was there, she may as well check out Spenser's General Store, too, browse around, and pick up a magazine or paperback.

"Wahoo," she murmured wryly. She was definitely in for a busy, fun-packed evening.

The café was in the opposite direction of Lucky's ranch, but just as far away from Mrs. Yancy's. Saddlers Prairie might be a small town, but it sure was spread out.

As usual, the highway was mostly deserted, and the road was all hers. The sun edged slowly toward the horizon, tinting the vast sky in spectacular pinks and golds.

Talk about your romantic evening.

Sarah's unwitting thoughts turned straight to Clay. He probably had a date tonight with some adoring woman.

She pictured him with a tall, voluptuous female who hung on his every word. Would he take her out someplace, or would they stay in and create their own private entertainment?

Not at all happy with the thought, Sarah frowned and pressed down hard on the accelerator. The car shot forward.

In the distance, pulled off to the side of the road, a deputy stood with a radar gun pointed at her. She quickly slowed to the speed limit. As she passed the deputy she waved and smiled.

Then her mind homed right back to Clay. She didn't want to think of him kissing or doing other things with some other woman, but she didn't want him kissing *her,* either.

"So what exactly *do* I want?" she asked out loud.

The answer popped instantly into her head, as if it had been waiting for the question. She wanted a man to love and build a family with.

"I'll start looking for him," she promised out loud. "Just as soon as I find Tammy Becker."

A road sign indicated that the exit for Spenser's General Store and Barb's Café was just ahead.

Sarah pulled into a pockmarked lot that looked full. She didn't see any parking spaces. Well, it *was* Saturday night.

Stomach growling, she cruised around at a snail's pace, searching for an empty slot. Suddenly her cell phone rang. She glanced at the screen. Private caller. It had to be Clay.

Of all people. He must not be out on a date, after all. Maybe he wanted to see her tonight. Why else would he call during the dinner hour?

If he thought she was one of those women who waited around for him to ask her out, and then came running, he was wrong.

She almost let the call go to voice mail, but in the end, she slipped on her Bluetooth. "Hi, Clay."

"Hey," he replied in his smoky voice.

Her heartbeat accelerated, and unwanted warmth flooded her.

"Find anything unexpected in the footlocker?" he asked.

They hadn't spoken since she'd taken it with her to Mrs. Yancy's. Since then only two days had passed, but it felt like forever.

"Nothing that answers any of my questions." She sighed. "Yesterday I drove over to Four City High School." She told him about the fire and the loss of school records. "I also contacted the local church in

Saddlers Prairie, and I tried some of the others outside town. Unfortunately, I came up empty. It's hard not to get discouraged."

"I'll bet. I hear music. You at a bar?"

"By myself? That's my car radio." She laughed and turned down the volume. "I'm in the parking lot for Spenser's and Barb's Café, trying to find a place to park. What's up?"

"Maybe you should find that parking space first."

Sarah sensed the undercurrent in his tone and *knew*. Clay had found out something about Tammy. Forget about dinner. She hit the brakes. "Tell me now," she said, too impatient to wait.

"Suit yourself. I was out having a beer and burger earlier, when the bartender mentioned the Beckers. He's met people by that name. They live in the same retirement home as his great aunt. He isn't sure they're the Beckers you're looking for, though."

Sarah's heart stuttered. "But they might be."

"It's definitely worth checking out. These people could be your grandparents."

Grandparents. Sarah hugged herself. "Did the bartender mention Tammy?"

"No, but he doesn't really know the Beckers."

"What's the name of the place where they live?" she asked, exhilarated and hopeful that this tip would pan out.

"It's called Sunset Manor. I checked the address online, and it's roughly twenty-five miles northwest of town."

"That's so close," she breathed.

If they were the right Beckers, she could meet her biological grandmother and grandfather. They would tell her where Tammy was, and hopefully the name of her biological father.

Behind her, a car honked. She was so keyed up that she almost had a heart attack. "Hold on, will you?" Luck was with her, and she found a spot at the back of the lot. "Okay, I'm parked now. Who did you say told you?"

"A bartender at Sparky's, a tavern on the edge of town. He heard through the grapevine that you were looking for the Beckers. Don't ask me from who. In this town, it could be anybody."

"Probably Mrs. Yancy."

"Ah, Mrs. Yappy."

Sarah sensed Clay's smile and couldn't stop one of her own. "I like her, Clay."

"I know. Back to the Beckers at Sunset Manor. Are you going to contact them?"

Sarah had planned to spend Sunday driving around and snapping photos for her article. But if her grandparents wanted to see her instead… "Of course. I'll call them right away."

Too jazzed to sit still, she exited the car and paced the lot.

A few curious people glanced her way. She could no more stop the happy grin on her face than stop breathing, and couldn't help but notice the responding smiles. Saddlers Prairie really was a friendly place.

"I'll keep my fingers crossed that they're your grandparents," Clay said.

"Please do. Thank you so much for letting me know. By the way, I spent this afternoon with a rancher you might know, Lucky Arnett."

"Lucky's a good guy, and he sure knows his way around cattle and ranching."

"So does his foreman, Zach Horton."

"I've met Zach."

Something in Clay's tone caught her attention. "You have something against him?" she guessed.

"Zach's all right. What do *you* think of him?"

"He seems smart and competent, and he answered all my questions."

"Did he ask you out?"

The question startled her. "Not that it's any of your business, but no. Ours was a purely professional meeting, Clay. An interview."

"I'm familiar with your interviews," he said drily. "As I recall, you and I stretched the definition of professional quite a bit."

Her face heated. She lowered her voice and turned away from a youngish couple watching her with interest. "That was different. You and I were together hours every day, for a week and a half. I spent maybe an hour with Zach. We didn't connect the way you and I did."

"You're saying you felt something for me back then."

If she hadn't, she never would have spent all those hours fantasizing about building a relationship and a future with him. She wouldn't have kissed him, wouldn't have dreamed about him for years.

"You *did*," he said.

"It was a long time ago, Clay."

"Not that long. You felt something," he repeated.

What was the point of denying it? "All right, I admit it."

He made a satisfied sound, and she could almost see his triumphant expression.

"Your ego is showing," she said.

"My ego has nothing to do with this. I've always wondered."

Sarah just bet. "Now you know. I should go."

"Let me know what happens with the Beckers."

"Okay, but would you mind explaining why you're so interested?"

"Because when you shared Tammy's journal and other stuff with me, you hooked me in, Sarah, better than the suspense novel I'm reading. I'm vested in your life now, and when you finally connect with your blood relatives, I want to know."

He sounded so earnest and heartfelt, that then and there she forgave him for his big ego and just about melted.

"My friends back home haven't exactly been enthusiastic about my search for family, and your interest and support mean a lot," she said. "Sitting with me and listening while I sorted through the footlocker the other day—that went above and beyond, and I really appreciate it."

"Like I said, I enjoyed it—*all* of it."

The longing that had been with Sarah since those intense kisses that day flared up inside her, and she knew that if Clay were with her now, she'd step into his arms for more.

Which would be a total mistake. Thank goodness she was nowhere near him.

Clay cleared his throat. "I'll let you go eat now. Good luck with that call."

HE REALLY NEEDED a sign letting people know that this was Hollyer Ranch, Clay thought as he parked at the ranch early Sunday afternoon. Something to take care of later. The construction crew took Sundays off, and no one was there. No hammering, sawing or radio music to disturb the quiet. Birds called to one another and squirrels raced back and forth, chattering playfully.

Nothing had changed since yesterday, when he'd interviewed and hired half a dozen of the experienced hands who'd worked with Mattson. Some of the framing was up. Not enough to make sense of the size and scope of the house, but progress all the same.

The house was coming together. Burl had moved into his cottage yesterday, and the other ranch hands were moving into their trailers sometime today. First thing tomorrow, they'd get to work on repairing or replacing fencing, while Burl evaluated the equipment that had come with the ranch.

If all went well with that, Clay and Mattson would check out the cattle auction on Wednesday. Once Clay purchased a suitable herd and the business was up and running, he would contact and visit rodeo producers across the West.

After enduring eighteen months of physical pain and mental anguish, when it seemed that his life had tanked and nothing would ever change, things were finally coming together.

Feeling upbeat, he limped around the ranch as he did every Sunday, visualizing his pastures alive with animals and a busy crew and the sounds of a working ranch.

A pleasurable way to pass the time. Today though, he was restless, and he knew who was to blame. Sarah Tigarden.

That phone call last night… Clay shook his head. She'd been so excited and had sucked him right in with her. His mind filled in the physical details—her blue eyes extra wide and bright, her cheeks flushed, her lips parted a fraction….

The mental image was enough to drive a man crazy,

and he'd come this close to inviting himself to join her at Barb's, just to see if he'd fantasized her right.

More than that, he'd wanted to be with her, wanted to hold and kiss her, and show her a whole different kind of excitement.

His body began to stir and predictably hardened. Clay frowned. Before the accident, life had been simpler. When he wanted a woman and she wanted him, they got down to business and enjoyed themselves. Since than, two things had changed—he'd given up mindless sex, and the group of willing women he'd once taken for granted had moved on.

A few had contacted him via email, asking to come visit. Clay never emailed back. He didn't want them around, didn't want the pity that was bound to be in their eyes.

Sarah didn't pity him. When he kissed her, she responded in a way that let him know she wanted him.

The rest of the time, he wasn't at all sure where he stood. One minute she was warm and sweet, and the next she acted as if she wanted to wring his neck.

It was confusing as hell, and figuring her out was proving to be as difficult as gauging an unpredictable bull.

Take that phone call she'd promised him after she contacted the Beckers. Clay hadn't heard from her, which could mean a number of things. They were the wrong Beckers, or she hadn't been able to get in touch with them. Or she had, and they didn't want anything to do with her.

Or she'd changed her mind and didn't want to keep him posted.

"Women," Clay muttered, scrubbing his hand over his face.

He was better off keeping his nose out of her business and staying away from her.

He started for the pickup, the rest of the afternoon and evening stretching out before him as endless as the Montana sky. He was rolling slowly down the driveway, considering a drive to the nearest town with a movie theater, some forty miles away, when a pale green sedan hummed down the highway. Sarah's car.

Clay honked and pulled onto the road behind her. She didn't seem to notice him or hear the horn. After checking for traffic and finding none, he pulled into the wrong lane so that the pickup was beside hers and honked again.

She startled and braked to a stop. Loud rock-and-roll music spilled through the sunroof. She adjusted the sound and pulled off her sunglasses. Shooting him a dirty look, she lowered her window.

"You scared me, Clay!"

"I honked, but you didn't hear me." He noticed a truck heading toward them. "There's a dirt turnaround about ten yards up the road. I'll meet you there."

A few minutes later, he pulled in behind her and exited the pickup. A light wind whispered through the prairie grass.

Clay leaned into her open window. "How'd the call go?"

"Call?"

She was wearing those sunglasses again, and he couldn't see her eyes. She slid her hands over the steering wheel, reminding him of the way she'd moved her palms over his chest before she kissed him.

Clearing his throat, he glanced at those impenetrable sunglasses. "The one you were going to make to the Beckers."

"Oh, that. Mrs. Yancy talked to a friend who confirmed that the same Bob and Judy Becker who used to live in Saddlers Prairie are now residing at Sunset Manor. They are my grandparents."

"But you didn't call them."

"I decided to surprise them instead. I'm on my way to Sunset Manor now, with my birth certificate and a few of Tammy's things."

"What if they aren't home? Twenty-five miles is a long way to drive, only to discover that the people you want to see are out," Clay said. "Or they could have company, or hell, they might even be asleep. It's been what, thirty years? If it were me, I'd want time to get used to the idea of meeting you. Otherwise, you don't know how they'll react to the shock."

"I'd rather just take my chances. If they're not at home, I'll write them a letter. At least the drive will give me a chance to get a feel for the area."

Her fingers nervously drummed on the steering wheel, and he finally understood. "You're afraid to call them."

Sarah released a loud sigh and looked up at him with a stricken expression. "Am I that transparent?"

"Afraid so."

"I thought about this most of the night, Clay. If I drop in unannounced, they can't hang up on me or lie and say they're busy, or that no, they don't want any contact with me. They'll have to meet me, and with any luck, they'll like me."

Her quick, fleeting smile only underlined her misgivings.

Clay gently tugged off the sunglasses so that he could see her worried eyes. "They've probably thought about you all these years, wondering how you turned out," he assured, smoothing her bangs. "Once they see how pretty and smart you are, and how easy you are to talk to, they'll be happy to know you."

Her whole face brightened. "You really think so?"

"I sure would."

"I appreciate the vote of confidence, but what if you're wrong?"

He hoped to hell he wasn't. That kind of rejection would hurt like the devil, and Sarah deserved better. "Sure you don't want to call them first?"

She looked terrified by the thought. "I just can't."

He was going to let her go, but his mouth jumped ahead of his brain, and he found himself asking, "Why don't I come along?"

"You've already done enough for me. Besides, I'm sure you have better things to do with your Sunday afternoon."

"Hey, if I didn't want to come, I wouldn't offer."

She hesitated. "Well, if you really want to…"

Realizing he'd been holding his breath, he exhaled. "Good. My ranch is about a half mile behind us. Why don't you leave your car there and let me drive."

Chapter Eight

Clay pulled up the gravel driveway of his ranch with Sarah following, and wondered what he was doing, bringing her here.

He gestured for her to park. By the time she exited her car and headed toward him, he'd nosed his pickup around to face the highway and stood waiting at the open passenger door.

She headed purposefully toward him, the skirt of her little sleeveless dress swinging and her strappy sandals kicking up dust.

"I like that dress," he said, letting his gaze rove lazily from her smooth shoulders and round breasts to her shapely legs and slender ankles.

"Thanks," she said, flushing a little. "I wanted to look nice." She glanced around. "So this is your ranch. It looks huge."

"Four hundred acres," Clay said, and tried to see the property through her eyes. The foundation and partially framed house, the dirt mounds, the stacks of building supplies and the sags and gaps in the fencing didn't look like much. "I finally hired a crew, and with any luck, I'll be buying my first stock on Wednesday."

Wanting to impress her, he pointed out areas of the ranch and described what he intended to do.

"It all sounds wonderful, Clay!" she exclaimed. She glanced at the construction. "I assume this will be your house."

He nodded. "It should be finished around Thanksgiving—if Ms. Nature cooperates and we don't get an early blizzard or some other natural disaster."

"And if Ms. Nature refuses to cooperate?"

"I'm working on ways to pay her off so that she will."

She smiled at his little joke, and he relaxed. Going with her was a good idea. He gestured toward the pickup. "Let's head out."

Instead of climbing in, she started fidgeting, twisting her hands together, kicking a pebble from her shoe. "I never heard of a stock contractor until the other day. Tell me how that works."

He saw right through her. "Putting off the meeting with your grandparents a little while longer won't make it any easier," he said. "I'll tell you about the business on the drive over."

With a reluctant sigh, she nodded and stepped up into the passenger seat.

Clay caught a flash of the creamy backs of her thighs before she slid onto the seat. Her shoulders weren't the only part of her body that looked smooth and soft.

Swallowing, he shut the door and headed around the truck, toward the driver's seat. Masking a wince, he climbed in.

"Mind if I change the radio station?" she asked as he pulled onto the highway.

No longer interested in the agricultural talk show he'd found, he shook his head. "Be my guest."

She found the country music station he liked. Toby Keith was singing "As Good As I Once Was," a song Clay could relate to.

"You were going to tell me about stock contractors," Sarah reminded him.

"There are a couple of different kinds," he said. "Some contractors produce rodeos and supply stock. "I'm not interested in the production side. Hollyer Ranch will focus solely on breeding and raising bulls and other cattle for rodeos. We'll also maintain a small herd of heifers and cows strictly for breeding purposes."

"I learned from Lucky that a heifer is a cow that hasn't had any calves yet," Sarah said.

"That's right. Most rodeo owners rent the stock for their shows, but sometimes they want to purchase an animal. That will be possible, too. The details will be worked out in a legal contract."

"I've never even thought about all that. The subject certainly never came up during those ten days I spent with you." A self-deprecating smile touched her lips. "But then, I didn't ask."

"Why would you? Your article was about me, not what goes on behind the scenes." Clay shrugged. "There's a lot about rodeoing that most people don't know about, some of it controversial."

She angled her head and frowned slightly, like she did when something puzzled her. "Controversial?"

Clay nodded. "Some contractors are known for treating their animals cruelly. Electric prods, sharpened spurs, bucking straps—those things make cattle and horses act crazy wild. Rodeo crowds like that, but I'm totally against it."

"Me, too." Sarah looked as outraged by that as Clay was. "Did using one of those awful devices cause the accident that crushed your knee?"

So she knew about his knee. He figured someone in town had told her, or maybe she'd checked online. He shook his head. "I'd gotten some bad news and was pre-occupied." He didn't intend to say another word about it, but the words came out anyway. "It was just before the event that the woman I told you about, the one who read your article, hit me with the news that she was pregnant and swore I was the father. I was pretty rattled. The bull didn't have to work very hard to toss me."

Sarah's eyes were huge. "I am so sorry, Clay."

"I don't want your pity. Anyway, that's all behind me now. I've moved on." At least he was trying. He was still adjusting to the unexpected end of his career. "Back to animal cruelty on the rodeo circuit. You can bet I'll make sure that none of my stock will ever be exposed to electric shock, bucking straps or sharpened spurs. That will be spelled out plainly in the contract, and someone from my operation will be present at every rodeo to make sure of it."

Sarah's sweet smile made his chest swell. "Your animals will be grateful. Let's say a rodeo producer wants to rent some of your bulls. Do you just pick any old bull that looks mean? How do you know a bull will buck like it's supposed to?"

"Crossbred Brahmans are a good choice because— wait a minute." Suddenly suspicious, he narrowed his eyes. "This is starting to sound like an interview. I told you, the answer is no."

She looked surprised. "I'm just interested, I swear." Her hands were laced together, the thumbs tapping each other. "I'm nervous about meeting the Beckers, and I guess I slipped into what I'm most comfortable with— interview mode."

Clay could only guess at how she felt, but he knew something about the jitters. "When I first started bull riding, I used to throw up before every ride," he admitted. "Even at the height my career, I sometimes still did."

"You?" Sarah scoffed. "I don't believe it."

"It's true."

"That's another thing you never mentioned before."

"I didn't think it was important."

"Of course it's important! Inquiring fans always want to know."

"Not about that. They expect a bull rider to be strong and tough."

Her eyes widened. "Ah, you didn't want them to know."

"Damn straight, I didn't. Any sign of weakness and they forget you ever existed." Clay had learned that the hard way, after his accident.

"But what you call weakness makes you human. People still love you, Clay. They always will."

She didn't know what the hell she was talking about, and he wasn't about to enlighten her. He gave her a quelling look. "Do you want to know how I dealt with the problem or not?"

Sarah nodded, and he went on. "A few months into my career, an old handler I knew caught me puking up my guts."

Clay remembered that afternoon as if it was yesterday. He'd been on his knees in a stall in the men's room, hugging the commode. In his haste to reach the toilet in time, he hadn't locked the door, and the handler had jerked it open, startling him.

"He thought I was drunk or hungover, but when he discovered I wasn't, he taught me a neat trick that helped me calm down," Clay said. "A technique I've used ever since."

"I could use something like that about now. Please, tell me your trick."

"It's called meditation."

"You *meditate?*"

Her astonishment irked him, and he raised an eyebrow. "You don't think I'm capable of quieting my mind and body."

"It isn't that at all. It's just…you don't strike me as a man who does that kind of thing."

Clay eyed her. "What kind of man *do* I strike you as?"

"The kind who works off nervous energy with physical activity. You know, pacing or jogging or riding."

"I use those when I can. But there are times when moving around isn't possible or isn't enough. Meditation requires no extra space, and once you learn how to quiet and clear your mind, it always works."

"Teach me," she said.

"I will, but not right now." He lifted the corner of his mouth. "It's not a good idea to meditate when you drive."

"Well, shoot. You wouldn't happen to have a stiff drink on you, would you?"

Clay chuckled. "Nope."

"Then I guess I'm stuck with this kaleidoscope of butterflies in my stomach." Within minutes, she knotted her hands together in her lap and grew so uptight that tension radiated from her.

Clay changed his mind. "I guess I can give you a few pointers that will help you relax."

"Anything that will help."

He shut the off the radio. "Take your shoes off and put your feet flat on the floor, then sit back and get comfy."

He waited for her to slip out of her sandals and settle in her seat before continuing. "Now, close your eyes. Take a slow, deep breath. Hold it, then exhale, pushing out all the air, until every ounce of it is gone. Then breathe in again and exhale the same way. Do it three times."

Sarah followed his instructions. Keeping his eyes on the road and his voice low and easy, he said, "Now, I want you to relax every part of your body. We'll start with your feet."

As he directed her through releasing the tension, he moved slowly from her calves to her thighs. That's where things got a lot more interesting.

While she was relaxing, Clay imagined getting rid of her anxieties in a whole different way. Stroking the soft skin of her inner thighs until her legs widened in silent invitation. Inching his hands higher, and...

Predictably, a certain part of his body woke up. He frowned. What in hell was he doing? Sarah needed his help. She wouldn't appreciate his thinking at all.

He forced himself to focus on helping her get calm, talking her through relaxing her stomach, then her back. "Now, relax your chest muscles," he said, glancing at her breasts.

Her dress wasn't tight or low cut, but the sweet hint of her hidden curves tempted him all the same. Clay started to get hard. Sneering at himself, he shifted in his seat.

"Pull in a deep breath through your nose," he said gruffly.

She opened one eye. "You're irritated."

"I'm fine," he said, willing her not to glance at his lap. "Close your eyes again."

"That's okay. That was fun, and I feel a lot more relaxed now."

Clay was the opposite, but her grateful smile was worth the discomfort. "I can tell," he said. "There's a calmness about you that was missing before."

"Thanks to you." She laughed and shook her head. "It seems that I'm always thanking you for something."

It had been a while since Clay had been appreciated by someone who didn't want anything from him, and he soaked up her gratitude. "No problem."

Sarah turned the radio back on, and music again filled the car. Eyes closed, head against the headrest, she hummed along.

Her long neck and decisive chin gave her a regal air, and at the same time, the slight, upward curve at the tip of her delicate nose was almost pixielike.

A beautiful combination. Sarah was beautiful, and the more her knew about her the more he liked her. He knew better than to trust her, but he sure wanted her.

Suddenly she glanced at him. "Tell me more about your family."

"You've heard about mom and dad, my sister, Lisa, and my nieces, Madison and Fiona. Lisa's husband, Chris, is a great guy."

"Are your parents still running the hotel in Billings?"

He nodded. "Lisa and Chris help run it, and our grandparents take turns at the front desk. It's pretty much a whole-family operation."

"Except for you."

"Except for me. The hospitality business isn't my thing."

"Do they mind that you bought a ranch in Saddlers Prairie?"

"Not at all. They just want me to be happy." Clay counted himself lucky for that.

Sarah looked wistful. "You're fortunate to have them, Clay."

"I am." Knowing what Sarah was going through made that all the more clear.

"Do you miss not living near them?"

At one time, he would've. The accident had changed that. His mom had wanted him to move back home, so that she could take care of him while he recovered. Clay knew she loved him, but he'd seen the resignation and pity in her eyes.

He didn't want or need either. Besides, he was a grown man, with good insurance, and thanks to a solid investment strategy, plenty of money. He'd hired a full-time nurse instead, and as soon as he was out of the chair and walking again, he'd moved to Saddlers Prairie.

"We email and talk on the phone, and try to Skype once a month," he said. "As a stock contractor I'll be traveling to rodeo organizations all over the western U.S., including Billings, and I'll see them then. And after the house is built, they can come down and stay with me anytime." He pointed out the window. "See that big building up there on the right? I'm pretty sure that's Sunset Manor."

Sarah nodded and reverted back to her tense pose. No traces of relaxed calm now.

Clay pulled into the crowded parking lot of a modern-looking structure with neatly manicured grounds. People of all ages strolled the gardens, and in the white gazebo nearby, a large group of people had gathered for what appeared to be a party.

Sunset Manor didn't look at all like the drab, stodgy place he'd imagined.

"Lots of people out and about today," he said. "But then, it is Sunday."

"I didn't think about that." Sarah swallowed. "What if Tammy and her family are here, visiting?"

With that, she dug into her purse for her comb and lipstick.

Clay reached for her cold hand. "It'll be fine, Sarah."

She looked doubtful, then squeezed her eyes shut, sucked in a breath, and nodded.

Not far from the entrance, he found a parking space. After shaking the kinks out of his bad leg, he headed around the pickup, where Sarah waited for him.

"How do I look?" she said, her face a mask of worry. "Is my hair okay?"

Aside from the anxiety radiating from her, she looked great. Clay made a show of brushing her bangs out of her eyes, just so he could touch her.

"You're beautiful," he said, his fingers lingering on the soft skin of her cheeks. He reached again for her hand. "Ready?"

She nodded, and together they approached the entrance to the building.

A BUNDLE OF nerves, Sarah moved hesitantly toward the glass doors of Sunset Manor and wished she'd called after all. If not for Clay's firm grip on her hand, she would have turned around and fled.

The doors slid open, and he tugged her inside a surprisingly airy lobby. Sunlight streamed through the skylights, shining on an abundance of lush, green plants.

Neither the decor nor the soft music meant to welcome visitors helped her dry throat and hammering heart.

"Courage," Clay murmured, squeezing her fingers. "Remember to breathe."

She inhaled deeply. At the front desk, an attractive girl with a name tag identifying her as Janine, was doing paperwork of some kind. She looked twenty— maybe it was homework.

"Hel—" Sarah cleared her throat. "Hello. We're here to see Bob and Judy Becker."

Janine peered up at her. "Are they expecting you?"

"No."

"Who should I say is here?" she said, reaching for the house phone.

At a loss, Sarah glanced at Clay.

"We'd kinda like to surprise them," he said, flashing his smile.

Busy looking up the Becker's phone number, Janine missed the smile. "For security purposes, I need to know who you are," she said, finally looking up.

Clay made a gesture of tipping his hat, only without the hat. "The name's Clay Hollyer."

The receptionist's eyes widened. "I *knew* you looked familiar."

The corner of his mouth lifted in its famous quirk.

Clearly overcome by the sight of the big handsome man standing within reach, Janine fanned herself. "*Clay Hollyer* is here," she announced in a voice loud enough for people in Alaska to hear. "He's at my desk!"

Men and women, young and old, began to move toward him. "Uh-oh," he muttered under his breath.

He squared his shoulders and broke into the familiar grin Sarah had seen on Facebook and billboards and in magazines.

Everyone wanted to shake his hand, get his autograph and pose with him for a picture.

His smile never slipping, Clay shook, signed and posed. Only Sarah noted the strain underneath.

Clay didn't enjoy being the center of attention, which came as a surprise, something to think about later.

After what seemed like ages, the last of the adoring crowd shuffled off.

"I texted my boyfriend and all my friends about you," Janine said. "They think I'm kidding. Could I get your autograph, too, and a picture with your arm around me?" She handed her phone to Sarah.

After Sarah snapped a few photos, Clay leaned toward the starstruck girl. "Look, this visit is a surprise. Just tell us where the Beckers live and we'll knock on their door."

"I'm not supposed to."

"Not even for me?" He flashed another smile, this one amped up to killer level. "I won't tell, I promise."

Minutes later, Sarah and Clay stepped onto the elevator.

"I can't get over how you charmed her into changing her mind," she said as the door closed. "How you charmed *everyone*."

"Another trick of mine that's come in handy."

"I'll bet. You didn't enjoy the attention, though."

He gave her a sideways look. "You could tell?"

"Only because I really looked. Believe me, no one else noticed."

He blew out a breath. "That's a relief."

"So…have you always been like this? Pretending you love being in the spotlight, when you really don't?"

"Guilty as charged, but please, keep that to yourself."

"Your secret's safe with me." She pantomimed locking her lips. "If you never liked the attention, why did you take up bull riding?"

"Because I was good at it, I enjoyed the challenge and it paid well."

Crossing his arms and setting his jaw, he leaned against the elevator rail and studied the floor indicator, letting her know he was finished answering her questions.

Sarah stared at the carpet. Clay Hollyer wasn't at all the man she'd thought he was when she'd written the article about him.

An article she regretted more and more.

She was on the verge of apologizing when the elevator stopped at the third floor.

"We're here," Clay said.

The door opened, and her mind emptied of everything but her fear. She grabbed for his hand and held on tight. Just as he had before, he gently squeezed her fingers, providing the reassurance she needed.

"Apartment 325 is this way," he said, steering her around a corner.

"Do you think Tammy's visiting them today?" she asked in a low voice. "I wanted to ask Janine, but I was afraid that if I did, she'd start questioning me."

Clay pointed out a white door and the "Bob and Judy Becker" doorplate attached at eye level. "We're about to find out."

A humorous doormat sporting cats in various poses and a small table holding a vase of artificial flowers sat beside the door, welcoming visitors.

Sarah hesitated. Would the Beckers welcome her when they found out who she was? If not, then what?

After another encouraging squeeze, Clay let go of her. "You can do this."

"Right," she whispered. Her hand shook as she pressed the doorbell.

As the bolt unlocked, she sucked in a painfully tight breath.

Clay put his arm around her shoulders and spoke in a voice for her ears only. "Smile, honey. It's showtime."

Chapter Nine

The front door opened, and a tall man with a paunch and thinning gray hair glanced from Clay to Sarah. His eyes widened and he looked taken aback.

Trembling and grateful for Clay's support, Sarah pasted a pleasant smile on her face. "Um, hello. You don't know me, but I—"

"Who is it, Bob?" came a woman's voice from inside the apartment.

He glanced over his shoulder. "You'd better get over here."

A plump woman with ash-blond hair joined him. She was slightly shorter than Sarah, and wore a conservative, churchy-looking dress.

Like her husband, she also glanced from Clay to Sarah. Her mouth opened, and she touched her collarbone. "You're Clay Hollyer."

They were rodeo fans—that explained why their jaws were on the floor.

"That's right." Clay smiled. "May we come in?"

"Of course." The woman backed away from the door and nudged her husband to do the same.

Sarah barely had a chance to glance at the plastic-covered furniture in the tidy living room before Clay spoke again. "This is Sarah Tigarden."

He gave her a meaningful look. Sarah swallowed. "We've never met, but I've been looking for you since… when I was an infant, I was adopted. I…" What to say now? She took a deep breath and exhaled it. "I don't know how to tell you this, so I'll just come out and say it. I'm your granddaughter."

Shock registered on their faces and turned them both ashen. Bob placed his hand on the wall, as if his legs were about to give out, and Judy stepped behind him.

It wasn't the reaction Sarah hoped for, but deep down, she'd expected this. Feeling strangely numb and heavy, she stood frozen where she was. Clay moved behind her and cupped her shoulders. "If you don't believe her, take a look at her birth certificate."

Bob Becker finally found his voice. "Never mind that. After all this time, why are you here now?"

"I would've come sooner, only I just found out I was adopted. The private eye I hired traced Tammy—and you—to Saddlers Prairie." The couple looked puzzled, as if they didn't know who Tammy was, so Sarah explained. "Tammy Becker is my biological mother. Maybe I have the wrong Beckers?"

Mrs. Becker shook her head. "No, we're the ones you want. Are you and Clay married?"

Would that make a difference, make them want to know her? Sarah shook her head.

As if Clay sensed how close she was to falling apart, he shifted closer so that his chest was against her back. Grateful, she silently soaked up his solid warmth.

"You'll never guess how we found you," she babbled out of nervousness. "Clay is renting your old house until the builder finishes his custom home. He found a footlocker in the attic that belonged to Tammy." She dug into her shoulder purse and brought out the journal and yearbook. "These were inside it. I thought she'd want them back, but since I don't know where to find her..." Breaking off, she offered them to Mrs. Becker. "Will you tell me where she is?"

Instead of answering the question, her grandmother covered her mouth with both hands and her grandfather looked as if he were about to throw up. Neither seemed to want to touch Tammy's things. Or Sarah.

Knowing she'd made a terrible mistake by showing up without calling first, Sarah ducked out of Clay's grasp and backed toward the door. "I'll just leave these things on the side table for you to give Tammy, along with my card," she said.

Without waiting for the Beckers to open the door, Clay silently turned the knob and ushered her out.

CLAY STARED AT the door that had shut rudely behind him and Sarah. He thought about jerking it open and punching Bob Becker in the jaw or chewing him out, but losing his temper was not the way to handle this.

The couple was in shock—that was obvious. Still, there were no words for the cruelty he'd witnessed. The Beckers had treated Sarah worse than the meanest cowboys ever treated a bull.

"Those people are a real piece of work," he muttered, looping his arm around her.

Fine tremors shook her body, and he wondered if she'd make it to the elevator without falling to pieces.

She surprised him by pulling away.

"You okay?" he asked.

"Please—I can't talk about this right now." Compressing her lips, she entered the elevator and stared straight-ahead.

When the car reached the lobby, she exited with as

much poise and confidence as he'd ever witnessed. Holding her head high, she strode through the lobby ahead of him, even managed a smile and a wave at Janine on the way to the door.

Outside, Clay caught up with her. As soon as he unlocked the pickup, she climbed jerkily into the passenger seat.

If he wasn't mistaken, she was about to lose it.

He slid into his own seat and glanced warily at her. "What can I do to help?"

"Just get me out of here."

He pulled out of the lot and onto the highway in record time—just as the first tears escaped her eyes.

Clay didn't blame her, but nothing reduced him to helplessness like a crying woman. Figuring she might need his full attention, he pulled onto a narrow dirt road that meandered through a grassy field.

As he steered toward a stand of trees and more privacy, the pickup bounced over the uneven ground. Sarah didn't question his actions or even seem to notice, just continued to swipe angrily at her eyes and stare into space.

Clay pulled behind the trees and killed the engine. After pushing his seat back as far as it would go, he reached across the console and pulled her onto his lap. She didn't put up any resistance, just collapsed against him, undoing him with her silence and pain.

Not sure what to do, he clasped the back of her head and held her close. She let out a heartfelt sob and then began to cry in earnest.

Wondering whether to leave her alone or keep touching her, he went with his instincts, rubbing her back and murmuring comforting words.

His shirt got wet, but after a while the tears stopped.

Wishing he had a tissue, Clay offered her the dry tail of his shirt. For some reason that started her crying all over again.

"You're so n-nice to me," she blubbered. "Taking time from your afternoon to c-come with me today."

His chest hurting for her, he tipped her head up. "I'm glad I did."

After a long, soulful look into his eyes, she sniffled and straightened. "Where's my purse?"

"On the floor." He reached between the seats and handed it to her. The thing weighed a ton.

She pulled out a packet of tissues and blew her nose. Then she burrowed close and stayed there. Clay kissed the top of her head.

After a time, she again looked up at him. "They hated me." Her bottom lip trembled.

Clay rubbed his thumb across it. "Nobody could hate you, honey. Seeing you came as a shock they didn't handle very well, but give them time. They'll come around."

If they didn't, he would personally give them hell until they did.

Her mouth opened a fraction, soft, sweet and begging to be kissed. Desire hit him hard. Feeling like a bum for wanting her while she was upset, he shifted away a little. She scooted closer, her soft bottom teasing him until he was hard and throbbing. Fighting a groan, he cupped her hips, holding her still to stop the torture.

"Maybe I'll write them a letter or something, and apologize for not calling first," she said. "You were right about that, and deep down, I knew it." Her eyes were huge and forlorn, her lashes clumped and dark with tears, and her makeup smeared. "I just wish I'd listened and saved everyone the torture I just put us all through."

He couldn't erase her pain, but he could say something to ease it. "Don't beat yourself up, Sarah. You did what you thought best."

Clay meant to kiss her forehead, but she raised up and kissed his lips. The hunger simmering inside him roared to life, and he lost the last shred of control.

NEEDING TO FORGET the pain, Sarah wrapped her arms around Clay's broad shoulders and buried herself in the kiss.

His hands slipped under her hair and cupped the back of her head. Making a low sound in his throat, he slid his tongue into her mouth.

She lost herself in his smell, his taste, his demanding, urgent mouth.

His erection pressed against her bottom, proof of his desire.

But did he want Sarah, or simply a willing woman?

Refusing to let the doubt and insecurity stop her, she placed his hands on her breasts. Clay groaned and cupped her. Pleasure rushed through her, and any doubts about him and what she was doing with him faded.

The most sensitive part of her pulsed with need and grew damp. Desperate to forget the world and lose herself in the moment, she straddled his lap, so close that only her panties and his jeans separated them from joining. Clay raised his hips and thrust against her.

Dear God. Wanting to touch his skin, she opened the buttons of his shirt, kissed his chest and licked his flat nipples.

"Sarah," he said in a velvety, smoky voice that made her squirm with need.

She was panting now, and when he reached behind her and started to unzip her dress, she went giddy with anticipation.

Then he stilled and stopped.

Every cell in her body protested. "Please, Clay, I want this."

"No, you don't."

He helped her back to her seat and scrubbed his hand over his face. "I ache to be inside you, Sarah, you know I do." He glanced down at his fly, stretched to bursting from his erection. "But this is no way to make love. Not in the pickup in some field where anyone could come driving up the road, and not when you're hurting. Do it because you really want to, because you want me."

DANGEROUSLY CLOSE TO tears again—this time from humiliation—Sarah fastened her seat belt. Unable to look at Clay, she stared out the passenger window and fought to stay calm.

The pickup bumped over the rough prairie track, rattles and noises drowning out the tense silence. In need of distraction, she turned on the radio and amped up the volume. Through lowered lashes she glanced at Clay.

His hands were locked on the wheel, his eyes fixed on the road, and she knew he felt every bit as uncomfortable as she did.

If only she could sink through the bottom of the pickup and fade into the grass. Unfortunately that wasn't possible. For the next twenty-five miles, she was stuck there with him.

Her over-the-top behavior seemed as foreign to her as a walk on the moon. She'd never acted like this before, had never rushed into sex. Yet today she'd been eager to do just that. No, not eager, desperate.

If it wasn't for Clay pulling back before it was too late...

Beyond embarrassed, Sarah squeezed her eyes shut.

The Clay she knew from before would never have stopped—or, at least, she hadn't thought so. Had he changed over the past three years, or had the fame and popularity blinded her to the decent man underneath?

Either way, he'd just proved that he was one of the good guys, someone she could easily fall in love with. But right now, she didn't want love. She wasn't even ready to get involved with a man until she found Tammy Becker.

Besides, just because Clay had taken the high road today didn't mean he wanted to date her. Sarah was pretty sure he didn't.

Who knew what he must be thinking? But after the way she'd just behaved, she must seem like the neediest, most pathetic woman in the world. She wasn't—she was strong and independent, and a little bruised.

She owed Clay an apology.

As mortified as she was, she took a while to work up to saying the words. By then, he was pulling up to her car at his ranch. Time was running out.

"Thanks for the ride and for the moral support," she said.

"Anytime."

Mustering her courage, she looked at him straight-on. "You were right to stop us from making love."

He nodded. "When you're ready, you know where to find me."

His eyes, oh, his eyes. Liquid green, warm and hot. Her body hummed with desire, and it was all she could do not to climb back onto his lap. Not about to make the same mistake twice, she opened her door, jumped out and headed for her car.

She was miles down the road before she was able to draw an easy breath.

Chapter Ten

As backbreaking as fencing was, on Monday Clay welcomed the chance to work with his new crew. Repairing and mending fence was taxing enough for a fit man, and his bad leg throbbed and protested something fierce. He could handle that, but when his leg threatened to buckle after a few hours, he reluctantly threw up his hands. The men understood. Knowing that on Wednesday, Clay would bring home cattle from the auction, they worked long hours to finish this first chore at Hollyer Ranch.

Despite working only a few hours, blisters bloodied Clay's palms, and his back, arms and both legs hurt in places he never knew could ache. Bull riding taxed a man's strength, but so did ranch work.

Tuesday afternoon he left the ranch and drove to Spenser's to pick up feed for the cattle. He reached for the radio, wincing as his biceps protested. Shania Twain was singing a song about a party for two, the lyrics turning Clay's thoughts to Sarah.

It had been two days since he'd driven her to the disastrous meeting with her grandparents, two days since he'd stopped himself from making a big mistake. Because making love with Sarah when she was upset and hurting would've been just plain wrong.

His hungry body thought he was nuts. Every time

he thought about her passion and eagerness, her shiver when he palmed her breasts and her thighs around his hips while she straddled him—and lying in bed at night he thought about it a lot—he ended up aroused and painfully hard.

He was hard right now, dammit. He couldn't recall ever wanting a woman this much, and hoped like hell that when she was in a better place emotionally, she'd come to him to finish what they'd started.

Spenser's was less than a mile ahead. Clay needed to lose the erection. He turned his thoughts to tomorrow's auction, and by the time he pulled into the lot he was settled down.

Then he spotted Sarah's car.

Anticipation shot through him, hurtling his body into full throttle at the mere thought of seeing her. Man, he was in trouble.

He almost U-turned and headed out. Only the fact that he needed to pick up the cattle feed before tomorrow stopped him.

He was easing into a parking slot when he spotted her exiting Barb's Café with Cody Naylor and his very pregnant wife, Autumn. Sarah seemed to make friends quickly, much faster than Clay.

Mindful of his leg, he stepped gingerly out of the pickup. She must've sensed him staring, for suddenly she looked straight at him. Her footsteps faltered and her cheeks flamed. Before he knew it, he was walking toward her and her new pals, doing his damndest not to limp.

"Hey," he greeted Naylor and Autumn, before acknowledging Sarah with a nod.

Her lips fell an acre short of a smile.

Every bit as awkward, Clay turned to Autumn. "You look like you're ready to pop."

"I feel that way, too, but I just had a checkup. According to Dr. Mark, our little girl will arrive right on time, a whole ten days from now. I'll sure be glad when she finally gets here."

Cody gave his wife a tender look and put his arm around her. "We all will."

He was about the happiest man Clay had ever seen. Crazy in love with his wife.

What did that feel like? Clay had no idea.

"How's the ranch coming?" Cody asked.

"Not bad."

They discussed fencing and machinery, and Clay explained about the cattle auction in Red Deer. "I'm here to pick up feed for them now."

"They're sure to be hungry. How many head are you looking to buy?"

"Cody," Autumn said, interrupting. "I hate to put an end to this conversation, but I really need to sit down."

"Of course." Cody's nod included Clay and Sarah. "See you tomorrow, Sarah. Good luck with that auction, Clay."

The couple sauntered off, and Clay and Sarah were left alone.

After hemming and hawing and searching for something to say, he settled for the truth. "I've been thinking about you." In X-rated ways that would flush her cheeks scarlet if she guessed. "How're you doing?"

"Pretty well, thanks." Her gaze didn't quite meet his. "I'm learning tons about ranching. I had an interview with Adam and Drew Dawson this morning. They're both super nice, and so are their wives and kids. They answered all my questions and let me take a bunch of photos. Lucky was just as open. Both he and the Dawsons inherited their land from their father, but the two ranches are so different."

Clay nodded. "From what I hear, the Dawson Ranch turned a profit from day one."

More dead space. He scrubbed the back of his neck. It was time to say "see you around" and head for Spenser's. Instead, he just stood there.

"Adam Dawson is the one who told me about Cody and Autumn," Sarah said. "He thought I'd be interested in their ranch, which is a little different from the usual cattle ranch. It doubles as a foster home for boys.

"Cody has a ranch crew, but after school the boys work there, too." She bubbled on. "One of them is in community college, and the others plan to attend after high school. It sounds like a pretty amazing place. I'll get to see for myself tomorrow afternoon, around the time the boys get home from school."

Clay had visited the ranch and met the boys. "They're nice kids—you'll like them. You've been busy."

"I don't have much time in Saddlers Prairie and I need to make every minute count."

A good reminder that she wasn't here long.

He wanted to ask about Bob and Judy Becker, but decided not to. "How are you really doing?" he said instead.

She hesitated, clearly thinking about that. "Surviving. I'm pretty embarrassed about the other day. "

"All of it?" He glanced at her mouth before jerking his gaze upward.

She blushed. "Not all of it, no."

He almost got lost in her big blue eyes. Sweet Jesus, he wanted her. The urge to touch her was almost impossible to ignore.

Jerking his gaze away, he fisted his hands at his sides. The blisters on his palms smarted something fierce, and he latched on to the pain. Better that than the awful need gripping him.

"I'd best get that feed," he said. "Take care." ·

"You, too."

She moved rapidly away, as if she, too, needed to put as much space between them as possible. He didn't relax until her car pulled out of the parking lot.

"I CAN'T BELIEVE you've been here a whole week already," Mrs. Yancy said over breakfast Wednesday morning.

Sarah agreed. Time seemed to be passing so quickly. "I know. I feel so comfortable here. Having breakfast with you every morning is something I'll miss when I leave. The food is wonderful, and you're so easy to talk to."

She wouldn't miss Clay—or so she tried to tell herself. Running into him at Spenser's yesterday had undone all her efforts to push him from her mind. He'd looked work-weary and dusty, and so incredibly good. Her heart had all but lifted out of her chest, and she had to admit she'd lied to herself.

The truth was, he hadn't been out of her thoughts since she'd first knocked on his door a week ago.

"If you want to extend your visit, I'd love for you to stay longer," Mrs. Yancy said.

Sarah considered the idea, but the safest thing to do was leave and never look back. "I couldn't, but thanks." She refilled her mug and topped off Mrs. Yancy's. "May I ask you something?"

"Of course."

"The first time your son contacted his biological mother, was she happy to hear from him?"

"As I recall, she was stunned and needed a while to adjust before she welcomed him into her life." Mrs. Yancy gave Sarah a sympathetic look. "It will be the same with your grandparents. Don't forget, they have to break the news to Tammy, as well. I'll bet that, in time, they'll come around, and so will she."

Clay had said the same thing, but Sarah had her doubts. In the three days since she'd knocked on their door, she hadn't heard a word from them. Not that she expected to. Their message had been loud and clear: leave us alone and go back where you came from.

"I've been thinking about writing to them," she said. She'd started a letter twice, but gave up when she couldn't think of the right words. Which was odd for a writer. Not for the first time, she wished she could go back and redo the meeting with them. "If I ask, maybe they'll tell me where to find Tammy."

"You could do that, but why don't you wait a little bit. They have your card. Give them time, and they'll call."

"But waiting is hard." Sarah's attempt at a laugh failed miserably.

Mrs. Yancy sipped her coffee. "I'm glad Clay went with you. He seems like a good man."

He was. The best.

"That's a heavy sigh."

Sarah was thinking about confiding in Mrs. Yancy about her dangerous feelings for Clay, when her cell phone rang. She glanced at the screen and froze. "It's Bob Becker."

"I knew it! Don't just sit there, answer the phone."

Fully aware of the woman's close scrutiny, Sarah

picked up. After a few minutes she disconnected. "You said they'd call," she said. "How did you know?"

"Because you're family. What did they say?"

"They invited me to come over tomorrow." Still in shock, Sarah shook her head. "They actually sounded friendly."

"Didn't I tell you? All they needed was a little time to get used to the idea of meeting their granddaughter. Are you going to call Clay and let him know?"

At the subtle note of excitement in Mrs. Yancy's voice, Sarah frowned. "There's nothing between us."

Nothing she cared to share.

"Of course not." Mrs. Yancy brushed muffin crumbs from the table into her palm. "But he was there with you when you visited them the other day. He'll want to know that they called."

This was true. "You're right," Sarah said. "Excuse me a moment."

She moved to the living room, out of eavesdropping range, and punched in Clay's number. His phone rang and went to voice mail before she remembered—wasn't he at a cattle auction today?

She left a message. "It's Sarah. I heard from the Beckers."

As THE CATTLE trucks Clay had arranged to transport his new herd trundled onto the highway toward Saddlers Prairie, he clapped Mattson's shoulder. "We did well today—or you did."

The foreman shrugged. "I'd better—I've participated in stock auctions since I was a kid."

Clay yawned. He'd had no idea the event would be so time consuming or require such focus. The day had started shortly after dawn, with a twenty-mile drive to Red Deer and the auction grounds.

Roughly an hour before the event officially started, he and Mattson had checked over the stock that were kept in holding pens and decided which ones they wanted.

After the bidding finished and Clay settled up, an on-site vet had examined the cattle and immunized them, with Mattson explaining the whys and wherefores and educating Clay. He was grateful to his new foreman for teaching him things he otherwise wouldn't have known.

The more Clay got to know Burl Mattson, the more he liked him. He counted himself lucky to have hired the man. "Why don't we stop on the way home and grab a late lunch?" he suggested. "On me."

"I won't say no to that. Let me call Jess and tell him that the stock is on its way."

While Mattson made the call, Clay kept an eye out for a restaurant and congratulated himself on a day well spent. Owning stock at last felt good, another step toward building his business. Things were finally falling into place.

If only he could say the same thing about his personal life...

He nodded at a sign indicating fuel and food ahead. "Let's find a place to eat off this exit."

Minutes later, they slid into a booth at a restaurant. It was the middle of the afternoon, and the place was virtually empty.

A cute redhead with a flirty smile brought the menus.

"I'm Misty, and I'll be back shortly to take your order," she said, giving Clay a sultry look.

"She likes you," Mattson murmured as she moved away with her hips swaying.

With no thanks to Sarah Tigarden, Clay felt nothing but the mildest appreciation. "She smiled at you, too."

"There was a time when I'd have gone for her, but not anymore." Mattson pointed to the wedding band on his finger. "Tara is the best thing that ever happened to me, and I'm not about to muck up this marriage."

Clay wondered at the telling comment.

"The first time I married, I was eighteen," Mattson explained. "We didn't get along and divorced before my twentieth birthday. I didn't think about marriage again until I met Tara, when I was barely this side of forty. She was also divorced, and I had to chase her pretty hard to get her to even date me, let alone agree to be my wife. She has two great kids I love like they're my own."

"How long have you been married?"

"Three years. I never thought I'd find a woman who'd want me and hold my interest. Tara does both."

Mattson gave a satisfied smile Clay envied.

"Just you wait—one day, some pretty little filly will lasso you tight and pull you in. And you'll go willingly, like a lamb to slaughter." He chuckled.

"I don't know," Clay said. "I've had my share of girl-friends, but I've never really been in love."

"That could've been me talking. 'Course, I wasn't a big rodeo star like you. But if love happened for me, it could happen for you."

Clay's phone vibrated, reminding him that he'd silenced the ringer during the auction and had forgotten to turn the sound back on. He slid it from his hip pocket and checked the screen.

To his surprise, he saw that Sarah had called. His heart thudding, he listened to her message. So she'd heard from the Beckers. Unfortunately, he couldn't tell whether that was good or bad.

"You okay?" Mattson said, and Clay realized he was frowning.

"I'm not sure. When the waitress comes back, order me a soda, cheeseburger and fries."

He slipped on his sunglasses and stepped outside. Standing in the parking lot, he called Sarah. She didn't pick up. "It's me," he said when voice mail started. "Just got your message. Call me back."

He hung up and rejoined Mattson, in time to see the waitress saunter off with their order in hand.

The foreman eyed him. "That was a quick call."

"She didn't answer."

"She?"

Clay shrugged. "Sarah Tigarden. She's a writer who's in town, doing research for a story on ranching."

Mattson nodded. "Is she researching you?"

If kisses and caresses counted, then yeah, they'd been researching each other. Not nearly enough, though. Clay wanted much, much more.

"Not exactly," he said.

Mattson looked curious, but the waitress delivered the sodas and lingered at their table, chitchatting about the beautiful weather and the string of sunny days forecast for the rest of the week.

When she left, Clay steered the conversation to cattle and ranching and kept it there throughout lunch and the pie they ate for dessert. Mattson had plenty to say that Clay needed to learn, yet his mind wandered.

Sarah's grandparents had finally called. Clay wondered if Sarah had apologized for stopping by without calling, and whether they'd apologized for their rudeness. Maybe they'd invited her into their lives. He wanted Sarah to call him back with the details, wanted to know how she was dealing with this latest turn of events.

The waitress brought him the check, along with a slip of paper with her name and phone number.

She wasn't the first. Clay had never known what to do with numbers he hadn't asked for and didn't want. He stuffed the paper into his pocket.

Mattson's eyes widened. "Are you going to call her?"

Clay shook his head. "I'm tossing it in the next trash bin I find. Let's get out of here."

Chapter Eleven

Hours later, after making sure the cattle arrived at the ranch and were settled in, Clay steered his pickup toward the highway.

After the long day, his leg throbbed. He was bone weary, and his empty belly demanded food. Not in the mood for pizza or another burger, he headed for Spenser's.

He also checked his cell phone. No word yet from Sarah. Clay was beyond curious to hear what she had to say. Why the hell hadn't she called him back?

Spenser's was quiet, and in no time he was pulling out of the parking lot with his beer and sack of prepared food on the passenger seat.

On automatic pilot, he headed for the rental house. The rotisserie chicken he'd bought smelled so good his mouth watered. He could hardly wait to pop open a beer, plunk himself in front of the tube and dig in.

The pickup had other ideas and drove him straight to Mrs. Yancy's place. Her neighborhood was similar to his, a narrow little street of modest houses and big yards. Sarah's sedan was parked out front.

Clay told himself to drive on past and leave her alone, but moments later, he walked up the front steps and knocked on the door.

Mrs. Yancy answered. Her round face lit up, as though he was a friend she hadn't seen in too long, rather than a guy she'd met once or twice.

"Clay! What a pleasant surprise—and me about to go out. A friend has invited me to dinner, and I'm due at her house shortly. What can I do for you?"

What *was* he doing there? Clay scratched the back of his neck. "I'm looking for Sarah."

"You're in luck—she just got back from an interview. Please come in."

He wiped his boots on the welcome mat and stepped into a small entryway. Mrs. Yancy directed him to the living room and disappeared up a narrow flight of stairs.

Clay wandered into a room filled with overstuffed furniture covered in flowery material bright enough to make his head hurt.

In no time, Mrs. Yancy bustled down the stairs. "She'll be with you momentarily," she said. "Did I forget to ask you to sit down? Please do. Can I get you some iced tea or coffee?"

Clay shook his head. "I'm good, thanks."

He had no idea what to say, but the woman's constant chatter filled in the silence. By the time Sarah came down the stairs, he was seriously regretting ever knocking on the door.

"Hi." Her eyebrows rose in question.

"If I don't leave this minute I'll be late," Mrs. Yancy said. "Good night, you two. I made brownies for the dinner tonight, but I'm leaving some here. Help yourselves."

"Does that woman ever stop talking?" Clay muttered when she shut the door behind her.

"Not so far." Sarah smiled.

With that, he relaxed. "Have you eaten?"

She shook her head. "As a matter of fact, I was planning on going back to Barb's tonight. The food there is really good."

Clay agreed. He considered inviting himself along, but he didn't feel like going out. "I just picked up a roasted chicken, a six pack and some other stuff from Spenser's, and there's more than enough for two," he said. "How about we share it, and you tell me about that call from the Beckers."

After a brief hesitation, she nodded. "That sounds like a fair trade. Let's eat in the kitchen."

Relieved but not sure why, he exhaled the breath he'd been holding. "I'll get the food from the truck."

Whistling, he headed outside.

SOMEHOW, THE KITCHEN table seemed bigger when Sarah shared it with Mrs. Yancy. "I see what you mean about having bought enough for two," she said, impressed by the feast-size quantity of food Clay had set on the table between them.

But then, when she'd first met him three years ago he'd had the same big appetite. No matter what he ate, the lucky guy never seemed to gain weight. "It all looks really good."

So did Clay. A black T-shirt hugged his broad shoulders, and as he carved the chicken, his impressive biceps flexed.

"Pass me your plate," he said.

Sarah could hardly believe she was sharing a meal with him. Given her unwelcome feelings, she wasn't sure how smart that was. But Clay only wanted an update on the Beckers. That seemed harmless enough.

Except to murmur over the tantalizing aroma of the food, neither of them spoke again until they'd filled their plates and sampled the dishes. Sarah was hungry, and Clay attacked his meal with the gusto of a starving man.

"This is surprisingly good," she said.

"Sure beats my cooking." Clay forked up a large mouthful and chewed with relish.

"I'm a pretty good cook," she said. "But it's been a while since I felt like making anything."

"Why is that?"

"For the past year, I pretty much took care of my mother 24/7. I cooked her three meals a day—bland dishes she could digest. I didn't have the energy to cook anything different for myself, so I ate it, too." She made a face.

"I thought you said your parents had both passed."

"They have. Ellen—my mom—had ovarian cancer. When she started to go downhill, I moved back home to take care of her." Sarah glanced at her plate. "She died about six months ago."

"That recent?" Clay stopped eating. "You never said. I'm real sorry."

"Thanks."

He placed his hand over hers. The gesture and his warm, sympathy-filled expression unleashed a flurry of sorrow. She dipped her head.

"You okay?"

She pulled away and nodded.

"What about your dad? How long has he been gone?"

"Since I was ten."

"I never knew that, either, yet you know all about my family. Why didn't you tell me?"

"You never asked."

"Yes I did, three years ago. You didn't say much about yourself, just kept reminding me that the interview was about me, not you."

"Which was true," she said. Intent on getting a realistic look at Clay and his life, she'd wanted to keep the focus on him.

"Taking care of your dying mother couldn't have been easy."

"No, but someone had to, and I was her only family. Dutiful daughter that I was."

"You sound bitter."

"I am. Not because I took care of her, because she never told me that I was adopted."

He looked taken aback.

"She never said one word," Sarah said. "I found out when I discovered my birth certificate in her safe-deposit box." But she didn't want to talk about that, didn't want to stir up the anger and pain. "You went to the auction today, right?" she asked before returning to her meal.

Clay eyed her with a slight frown, but to her relief, let her change the subject.

"That's right, and I learned more than I ever thought I would about cattle weight, breeding and health issues."

He shared some of what he'd learned.

"You know a lot," she said, impressed.

"My foreman, Burl Mattson, gets most of the credit for that. Without his help, I wouldn't have known what to look for. Thanks to him, I now own rodeo stock. They're at the ranch now, settling in. My crew are keeping a careful eye on them."

"You move fast, cowboy."

"In some ways." His eyelids lowered a fraction, his hooded gaze all but screaming sexual attraction.

Sarah reacted viscerally, her body launching into chaos mode. The familiar longing she'd harbored and fought for so long swept through her.

No longer hungry, she pushed what was left of her meal around her plate and questioned her sanity for having dinner alone with Clay.

She would tell him about the phone call. Then he'd leave and she'd feel safe again. "You asked about the call I got from Beckers," she reminded him.

Clay's expression cooled considerably. "What did they say, and what did you say?" he asked with the keen interest he displayed whenever the subject came up.

"I only spoke with Bob." Referring to him as Grandpa didn't feel right or comfortable. "He was a lot friendlier. He explained that he and Judy were still in shock, and I apologized for not calling first. Then he invited me over tomorrow afternoon."

"You're going, right?"

"Definitely."

"You're turning that paper napkin into a shredded mess."

Sarah crumpled the pieces in her hand. "To tell you the truth, I'm nervous about seeing them again. Even more scared than I was before."

"If you want company…"

She shook her head. "I need to do this alone." Clay's plate and all the food containers were empty. Sarah slid her plate toward him. "If you're still hungry, finish this."

"You sure?"

"Believe me, I couldn't eat another bite."

"I want to know what happens tomorrow," he said, making short work of the remaining food. "I'll be at the ranch, but I'll have my phone with me, so call— anytime."

It was a command, not a suggestion. Sarah saluted. "Yes, sir."

Busy scraping the last crumb from her plate, he looked up and grinned. A wide, heart-stopping grin.

"Feel better now?" she asked, when he set his napkin aside and sat back.

"Much, but I could use some dessert. Mrs. Yancy mentioned brownies."

"I'm sure they're delicious. Do you want coffee to go with them?"

"I'd rather have a glass of milk."

That made her smile. "Brownies and milk—I haven't tried that since I was little. You pour the milk and I'll get the brownies."

When they were both seated at the table again, Clay raised his glass. "To tomorrow."

"Tomorrow."

He bit into his dessert and made a sound of sheer pleasure. "No wonder you put up with Mrs. Yancy's chatter. These are fantastic."

"You should see what I get for breakfast. Between the muffins, rolls, quiche and coffee cake, I swear I've gained five pounds."

"You look great to me."

Clay's long, appreciative gaze rekindled the heat inside her.

He helped himself to a second brownie. "You look like you want another, too."

Not if she wanted to be able to button her jeans. She shook her head. "Better not."

"One more little bite won't hurt." He broke off a chunk of his brownie and offered it to her.

Acutely aware of his warm, masculine fingers so close to her lips, Sarah quickly accepted the treat and sat back, out of reach.

Clay polished off the rest and drained his glass. "What are you smiling at?" he asked, wiping his mouth.

"You, enjoying your dessert."

"What can I say? I'm a lover of all things sweet." His gaze settled on her mouth.

Something made her catch her bottom lip between her teeth in the way she knew drove him wild. Clay's eyes darkened, and her heart rate accelerated.

"Sarah?" He turned her name into a question.

She couldn't look away.

Clay stood and reached for her hands. She could no more deny him than stop breathing. He pulled her up and brushed her bangs back with his thumbs, making her want things guaranteed to cause trouble.

She told herself to back away, but her legs refused to cooperate. He traced the lines of her face with his finger. Warmth spread through her, and she shifted closer—she simply couldn't help herself.

"Unless you stop me now, I'm going to kiss you," he said in a husky voice she'd never heard.

The last of her willpower waved a white flag of surrender, and she rose to meet him.

HOME, CLAY THOUGHT. Holding Sarah, he was home. He slid his hand under her hair and kissed her the way he'd wanted to since he'd walked through the door tonight. Deeply and passionately, holding nothing back.

Her lips were warm, soft and welcoming. She twined her arms round his neck. Hard and throbbing, he cupped her sweet behind, anchoring her against his groin.

Hooking her foot around his calf, she angled in closer.

Wow. He palmed her breasts and heard her breath hitch.

She slid her hands under his shirt and restlessly up his back. Blood roared in his head. The sofa was only a room away. Still kissing her, he backed her out of the kitchen. They sank together onto the cushions.

Her lips burned and branded him, erasing his thoughts, making him crazy. Breathing hard, he pulled away to unbutton her blouse.

The pink bra, a piece of lace that jailed her erect nipples, was both sweet and sexy at the same time. Swallowing, Clay again traced one nipple with his finger. Sarah shivered with pleasure. He barely touched the other breast when she pulled back.

Locking her gaze to his, she slipped out of the blouse, undid the bra and dropped it. Her breasts were small but perfect, and flushed with arousal.

She cupped her own breasts and offered them to him. "Touch me again, Clay."

Placing his hands around hers, he reverently licked one rosebud peak.

Her unfettered sounds of need and pleasure drove him wild, and he took his time tasting and enjoying both breasts. She was squirming now, and he moved lower, freeing the button of her slacks. A tug at her zipper brought it down, and she raised her hips so that he could remove them.

She wore tiny little panties the same color as the bra, panties barely big enough to cover her thatch. So damn sexy. His desire ramping up, Clay slid his hand inside the silky fabric.

She was wet between her legs. He touched her most sensitive place and entered her with his fingers. His erection jerked. He was on the verge of losing control, but he couldn't stop now. Not while Sarah was writhing against his hand. Before long, she moaned and climaxed.

His own body demanded the same release, but he wasn't about to make love with her on her landlady's sofa. As hard and aching as he was, in a strange way he felt satisfied, just knowing he'd pleasured her.

He kissed her mouth, then pulled away. "I enjoyed that."

"It was really good." Her gaze went straight to the strained fly of his jeans. "What about you?"

There was only one way to get the kind of relief he craved, and it wasn't happening tonight. He managed a wry smile. "I'll survive."

He retrieved Sarah's blouse and bra from the floor. She slipped into the blouse, but left the bra off. When she faced him again, he could easily make out her nipples. Her usually sleek hair was tousled and wild, her lips red and slightly swollen and her face flushed with desire.

He'd never seen a more beautiful woman. He bit back a groan. "I'd better go," he said. While he still could.

Looking dazed, she nodded.

He thought about asking her to stop by his place tomorrow night instead of calling to update him about her grandparents, but next time he kissed her, he wouldn't be able to stop.

"I'll talk to you tomorrow," he said at the door.

She stood in the doorway, silhouetted in the light, until he slid into the pickup and drove away.

IN THE LIVING room, Sarah flipped on Mrs. Yancy's TV. She couldn't have said what program was on. She was too distracted by what had happened tonight, too uneasy.

Make that afraid. Her strong feelings for Clay scared her.

Clasping a sofa pillow to her chest, she closed her eyes and relived his kisses and caresses. When he touched her and looked at her as if she was someone precious, someone he couldn't live without, he was irresistible.

Even if he was only interested in the sex.

But if that were true, why had he given her pleasure tonight without taking any himself? Surely that meant he cared.

Don't be a fool. He seemed interested now, maybe even thought he cared, but only a few days ago, he'd come right out and admitted that he didn't do serious.

Which was fine with Sarah. She certainly didn't want serious. Not now, and not with Clay.

Liar.

And that was the trouble. She cared a little too much, just as she had three years ago. Even more, now that she knew him better. She also knew better than to think he might feel the same way or want more than sex.

Clay was a great guy, but she'd learned her lesson. She wasn't about to make the same mistake twice.

Besides, she had other things to focus on—finding Tammy and writing the article. Getting to know her grandparents was right up there, too. She didn't have time for anything else.

Feeling better, she flipped off the TV and headed upstairs.

Chapter Twelve

"Hell of an afternoon," Mattson said as hail the size of marbles pummeled the barn roof. "Didn't that waitress yesterday say something about our good weather holding?"

Clay and the entire crew had spent the past hour herding the cattle toward the sheltering pens. Everyone but Clay and Mattson had left to change into dry clothes.

Clay's leg was killing him, and he was soaked and bruised from where the angry hail had pelted him. At least the stock were safe. After drying his face and hair with an old towel, he grabbed one of the rickety chairs the previous owner had left behind and sat down. He propped his boots on the knotty pine table and poured himself a cup of hot coffee from the thermos he'd brought with him.

Mattson was also toweling off.

"Don't you want to change clothes?" Clay asked over the deafening noise.

"I don't see the point. When the hail lets up, it'll still be pouring rain and I'll be going out there again to open those sheltering pens back up." Mattson pulled over another chair, sat down and unscrewed his own thermos.

Lapsing into silence, he sipped his coffee, leaving

Clay with his own thoughts. He checked his watch, surprised that it was after two. By now, Sarah would be at her grandparents'. He hoped like hell that this meeting went better than the last one.

He couldn't stop thinking about her, about last night. Her soft, flushed skin, the way her jagged breath caught and rushed, the shudder that had shaken her at her climax.

Predictably, his body revved up in what was starting to get really old. The thundering noise lessened, the hail slowing. Not wanting Mattson to catch sight of his hard-on, Clay removed his feet from the table, stood and wandered toward the open barn door.

By the time he reached it, the hail had stopped altogether, replaced by the driving rain Mattson had predicted.

"I'll open the doors to those sheltering pens," he said. "You go on to your cabin and change."

"You don't have to do that, boss. That's what you hired me for."

Clay welcomed the wet and cold as a chance to cool down. "Go on home and change, Burl. I'll take care of the doors, and then I'm heading out."

REGRETTING THAT SHE hadn't taken up Clay's offer and let him come with her, Sarah stepped off the elevator on the Beckers' floor. The hail and rain had made a shambles of her appearance, which only added to her bad case of nerves. She'd stopped in the ladies' room off the lobby to comb her hair and refresh her makeup, but no amount of grooming could chase away the butterflies in her stomach.

Coming toward her, an elderly man on his way someplace stopped. "You look like you're lost."

In a sense, she was. "I think I can find my way," she replied, forcing a smile.

She reached the door and raised her arm toward the doorbell. Dropped it and stood there, shaking in her ankle boots. "Breathe," she whispered to herself, just as Clay would have if he were with her.

After pulling in several deep breaths, she felt calmer. Yet seconds passed before she summoned the courage to ring the doorbell.

In a blink the doorknob turned, as if the person behind the door was standing there, waiting for her.

Bob Becker opened the door. This time, he almost smiled. "Come in, Sarah."

He led her to the fussy living room, where pleated linen drapes were closed against the ugly weather.

"Please, sit down," he said, gesturing at a plastic-covered arm chair.

Sarah perched on the edge of the crisp seat, her weight causing a faint crackling sound. "Thank you for inviting me over today, Mr.—um, what should I call you?"

"Mr. Becker or Bob—either one is fine."

At least he hadn't asked her to call him Grandpa. That would've felt way too awkward.

"My wife is the kitchen, fixing a snack tray. I'll let her know you're here."

As soon as he disappeared from the room, Sarah glanced around. Someone had set Tammy's yearbook and journal on one side of the otherwise empty coffee table. Straight-ahead, a cross and picture of Jesus hung on the off-white wall, and in the corner stood a bookcase containing figurines and a vase of artificial flowers that matched the ones outside the door. Aside from a Bible that appeared well used on a side table, there were no other books. The mantle over the fireplace held several photos of Mr. and Mrs. Becker, either just the two of them or with other couples, but Sarah saw none of a female Tammy's age.

She barely had time to wonder about that before Mrs. Becker entered the room with a coffeepot. Behind her, Bob carried a tray that looked heavy.

The older woman's smile wasn't quite as welcoming as her husband's. "Hello, Sarah."

The armchair crackled as Sarah shifted her weight. More uncomfortable than ever, she forced a smile of her own. "Hello, Mrs. Becker."

The couple sat down on the sofa across the coffee table. *Crackle.*

"My husband and I always enjoy a cup of coffee about now," Mrs. Becker said. "Would you care to join us?"

Just what Sarah needed to calm her nerves—caffeine. Stifling the urge to laugh hysterically, she instead nodded. "That would be lovely."

Lovely? Not a word she normally used. She sounded like Ellen.

Mrs. Becker arranged three porcelain cups and saucers on the coffee table in front of her. She filled each and then nudged one toward Sarah, along with a spoon. "Help yourself to the sugar and milk."

Sarah had barely tried a sip before the older woman held out a plate. "How about something to eat?"

The store-bought, cream-filled sandwich cookies didn't appeal to Sarah, especially with her stomach tied in knots. Still, she accepted one.

Mrs. Becker offered her husband the plate. After he piled a few on his saucer, she took some for herself and settled back. The two of them sipped their coffee and nibbled their cookies without any show of joy or interest.

Moments of awkward silence passed. Biting into her cookie just for something to do, Sarah wracked her brain for a topic of conversation.

"Did you—"

"We read through—"

She and Mrs. Becker said at the same time.

Sarah dipped her head. "Go ahead."

"When I saw you the other day, I felt as if I'd stepped back in time." The saucer in the older woman's hands trembled slightly, whether from nerves or some health issue, Sarah couldn't guess. "You look so much like her."

Sarah knew she meant Tammy. She nodded. "I noticed that when I saw her yearbook picture."

"Looking through the yearbook and reading her diary brought back so many memories," Bob said, his voice laden with feeling. "We had no idea any of Tammy's things were still in Saddlers Prairie."

"Clay found a whole trunk of hers in his attic. I'm guessing she'd like it back." Mrs. Becker paled, which puzzled Sarah. "If you think she'd be upset that I've found you, you don't have to tell her where you got them," she said.

"It isn't that. It's—" The woman broke off, set her coffee cup on the coffee table and gave her husband a helpless look.

He cleared his throat. "The truth is, we have no idea where our daughter is."

This was the last thing Sarah expected. She frowned. "Are you saying Tammy has disappeared?"

"Three days after you were born." He stared into space, as if seeing the past. "When you were two days old and Tammy was still in the hospital, the adoption people took you away. The next morning, I went to the hospital to pick Tammy up and bring her home, but she was already gone."

Mr. Becker swallowed audibly and bowed his head for a moment. Before continuing, he cleared his throat. "The hospital staff claimed her aunt had picked her up." He gave a bitter smile. "How were they to know she had no aunts?"

Mrs. Becker massaged the space above her heart, as if it hurt. "We never did find out who she left with or where they went. And we never learned who was responsible for the pregnancy. Tammy refused to give his name."

"We heard rumors that she changed her last name to Smith," her husband went on. "But we couldn't track the source of the rumor, and the information never panned out. We sold the house and spent the proceeds and most of our savings trying to find her, but after two years of nothing but false hopes and dead ends, we gave up."

Mrs. Becker's face remained impassive, but she wrung her hands incessantly. "I wanted to leave Montana and start fresh," she said. "But we prayed about it and decided that if and when Tammy wanted to find us, she'd come back to eastern Montana. That's why we stayed close to home all these years."

"In thirty years, she's never contacted you?" Sarah asked.

Mrs. Becker shook her head.

"You'd think that, after all this time, we'd have put it behind us." Pulling off his glasses, Mr. Becker rubbed the space between his eyes. "But when you knocked at the door, everything flooded back."

Witnessing the couple's distress put an ache in Sarah's chest. "I'm so sorry," she said, wishing again that she'd given them a call before showing up at their door.

Though they were probably only five years older than Mrs. Yancy, at the moment they both looked ancient. Sarah thought about wrapping them in a hug but didn't want to deal with their probable rejection.

"We've been wondering—how exactly did you find us?" Mr. Becker asked.

"I hired a private detective in Boise, a man named Pete Charles. His investigation led me to the house in Saddlers Prairie where you used to live with Tammy. After you sold the property and moved, the trail went cold. I even tried to find your church, but didn't have much luck."

Mr. Becker nodded. "That's because back in 1984, our pastor moved to Nevada and the congregation disbanded. Who did you say told you we were here?"

"Actually, Clay found that out from someone in town whose great aunt lives here. I didn't get any names."

"Did Pete Charles happen to find any record of Tammy?" Mrs. Becker asked hopefully.

Sarah shook her head. "Nothing after I was born. We didn't have her birth date or social security number, and like you said, she changed her last name. Without any of those things, locating her has been virtually impossible. That's why I came to Saddlers Prairie—to see what I could learn."

The couple shared a look, and Mrs. Becker nodded. "We can give you Tammy's birth date and social security number right now. I'll be right back with a pen and paper."

"No need—I'll store the information in my phone." Sarah input the information, and then put the phone away. "I'll contact Pete this afternoon."

Mrs. Becker bit her lip and glanced at the journal and yearbook. "Would you mind if we keep these?"

Having practically memorized the journal, Sarah shook her head. "When we find Tammy, you can give them to her."

"Thanks." No longer stoic, the older woman looked close to tears.

Sarah wasn't far from crying herself. It was time to leave. "I should go," she said, standing. "Thank you for inviting me over."

At the door, Mrs. Becker fussed with her hair. "Will you come back again?"

"I'd like to, but it'll have to be soon. I'm leaving next Wednesday." Six short days from now.

The woman's face fell. "But we only just met."

A thought flitted into Sarah's head, that when she sold the house in Boise, she'd move to Saddlers Prairie to be closer to her grandparents. Which meant she'd also be closer to Clay—but she wasn't going to think about that.

"Come for dinner tomorrow night," Mr. Becker said. "And bring Clay Hollyer along."

"Yes, bring Clay," his wife echoed. "He's your boy-friend, and we want to get to know him, too."

"We're not involved," Sarah said. Not unless you counted the kisses and more....

Her grandmother looked genuinely disappointed. "But I thought for sure...when you brought him along the other day...you make such a handsome couple, and you said he was the one who found out that we lived here. Are you sure you're not involved?"

Not in any way Sarah wanted to share. "We're friends," she said.

"Then by all means, invite him anyway. If he can't

make it, come by yourself. We've already missed too much of your life, and we have a lot of catching up to do."

A cloud seemed to lift from the room, and Sarah smiled. "I'll be here, and I'll get back to you about Clay. Should I bring anything? Appetizers, dessert, a bottle of wine?"

"No need. We'll eat in the dining room—I'll reserve a table. How about six-thirty?"

"Perfect. I'll see you then."

Sarah waited for some gesture of affection—a proffered cheek or a hand squeeze. None came. Like Ellen, the Beckers were reserved and unaffectionate.

Still, the afternoon had gone well, far better than Sarah had expected. Unable to wipe the smile from her face, she floated down the elevator and through the lobby.

BY THE TIME Sarah pushed through the Sunset Manor exit, the clouds had disappeared and the sun was bright and hot—as if the rain and hail had never happened. Overcome by her afternoon with the Beckers, and all that she'd learned, she barely noticed.

Shockingly, Tammy had run away and disappeared. Where had she gone, and where was she now? Sarah wanted answers, and not just for herself. Her grandparents needed to find their only child, and the three of them needed to make up with each other, before it was too late.

And didn't Sarah know. If only she could see Ellen one last time, clear the air and get rid of her bitterness.

Unfortunately, that was impossible. But the Beckers still had a chance to resolve their differences with Tammy.

Too emotional for the long drive just yet, Sarah wandered down a walkway across the landscaped grounds of the retirement complex, passing seniors of various ages out for a stroll.

After the storm, the air smelled sweet and fresh, and the peace and quiet were broken only by twittering birds and the occasional "hello" exchanged between her and people she met along the way.

As pleased as she was about this afternoon, Sarah also felt raw and shaky from the emotions swirling inside her. She wished she were seeing Clay tonight, so that she could hold on to him when she shared it all. His steady, solid strength and belief in her were exactly what she needed.

The concrete path looped around the grounds, and by the time she ambled toward the parking lot, she felt more in control of herself and ready to make phone calls.

The gazebo stood empty. Sliding her phone from her purse, she speed-dialed Pete Charles and entered the little building. The cushioned furniture looked inviting, but she was still too restless to sit. She leaned against the railing.

"The birth date and SSN should kick up some good leads," Pete replied after she supplied the information. "But the surname 'Smith' won't get us anywhere— nearly three million Americans share that name. It'd help if we knew what city and state Tammy lived in, but I'll see what I can find. Give me a day or two."

As soon as Sarah disconnected, she punched in Clay's number. He answered on the second ring.

"Hey," he said in that deep voice that made her knees go weak. "I've been wondering when you'd call. Are you already back in Saddlers Prairie?"

Sarah smiled and teared up at the same time. Apparently she wasn't in control of herself, after all. "No. At the moment, I'm standing in the gazebo at Sunset Manor." She swallowed hard. "And I'm feeling pretty emotional."

"Tell me."

With that, the whole story spilled out, starting with Mr. Becker opening the door and ending with the call to Pete Charles. "He's going to get back to me in a day or two," she said.

"Sounds promising."

"Keep your fingers crossed. My grandparents—they aren't expressive about their feelings, but they did ask me to dinner tomorrow. You're invited, too. They're making a reservation in the main dining room here for six-thirty."

"Me? Why would they want me there?"

"I guess because tomorrow's Friday night—date night—and Mrs. Becker thinks you're my boyfriend." Sarah laughed self-consciously.

Instead of laughing along, Clay remained serious. "What did you tell her?"

"That we aren't involved."

"But we are."

The air rang with the truth in that statement.

Regardless of what she'd told herself last night, there was something between her and Clay that couldn't be denied.

Sarah sank onto a love-seat rocker.

"I can't stop thinking about last night," he went on in a low, smoky voice that glided over her skin like a caress.

Her whole body hummed. Closing her eyes against a flood of need, she rocked herself back and forth, working to contain feelings she wasn't ready for—and failing.

Clay cleared his throat. "Sarah? Are you still there?"

"I'm here." To her own ears, her murmured reply sounded fevered, aroused.

"I wish I were with you now."

His tone was packed with meaning, and she almost swooned in anticipation. And knew then that, reckless or not, in the very near future, she and Clay would make love.

She stopped rocking and watched a male robin pluck a worm from the ground. "What should I tell my grandparents about dinner?"

"Let them know that I'll join you. I'll pick you up a little before six."

Chapter Thirteen

Freshly showered and wearing his good clothes, Clay crossed Mrs. Yancy's porch to the front door and wondered who'd open it this time.

After a hectic day at the ranch, his leg bothered him, but otherwise he felt okay. The thought of spending the evening with Sarah made him feel too happy for his own good.

He was also ready to eat a whole cow. His belly was that empty. Dinner should be interesting. He would see for himself how the Beckers treated Sarah.

He was even more interested in after dinner, when he hoped to be alone with her.

The sun was still fairly high in the sky and bright enough that he left his aviator sunglasses on as he rang the doorbell.

From inside, he heard footsteps too light to belong to Mrs. Yancy. Sarah opened the door.

"Hey," he said, enjoying her appreciation as she checked him out.

"You're wearing slacks and a sport coat."

"You said we were eating in the dining room. I brought a tie, too, just in case." He flipped up his shades and let his gaze flicker over her sleeveless, above-the-knee dress and strappy red sandals that were sexy as hell. "You dressed up, too. I like that outfit."

"Thanks."

The corners of her mouth curving a fraction, she stepped aside, letting him in. He smelled her perfume and her own natural scent underneath, and the need to kiss her flared in him.

"Where's Mrs. Yancy?" he asked, barely curbing his impatience.

"She went out again. I swear, that woman has a more active social life than I ever—"

Clay leaned in and kissed her, lingering until she released the soft sigh he'd begun to crave.

They needed to leave or they'd be late, and he intended to end the kiss. But she melted against him and wrapped her arms around his neck, and his mind blanked.

Sometime later, hard with desire, he pulled back. "I've been thinking about doing that all day."

"Me, too," she said, wearing a sweet, unfocused expression that about undid him.

If not for the dinner date with the Beckers, he'd have pulled her close again and forgotten all about food. But he wasn't about to get in the way of her first meal with her grandparents. "We should go," he said.

"Right." For a moment she looked confused, as if she'd forgotten where they were headed.

She grabbed her purse and a tiny little sweater she called a shrug, and they headed for the pickup. Unable to keep his hands off her, he cupped her bare shoulder and steered her forward. Her skin was soft, warm, supple. A surge of need shot through him, and he swallowed.

He helped her into the truck, enjoying the way her skirt hiked up her thighs when she slid into the seat.

"What did you do today?" he asked as he drove toward the highway.

"I met with two more ranchers and started organizing my notes. There's a lot of information to sort through. How was your day?"

"Busy. We spent most of it inseminating the heifers and cows with bull sperm."

She did a double take that was almost comical. "Pardon me?"

"That's how ranchers impregnate their cows."

She shook her head. "The things I learn from you. And here I thought they used a live bull."

"Trust me, some bulls prefer to do the work themselves. It's a lot more fun that way, both for them and their partners." He grinned and raised his eyebrows suggestively. "But the other way is faster and more efficient."

"You'd think one of the ranchers I interviewed would have mentioned that."

"They probably figured you knew."

"I wonder what else I'm missing by not knowing enough to ask," she said, sounding slightly put out.

Probably quite a bit. Clay had half a mind to agree to let her interview him for her ranching article. But as much as he liked and wanted her, he didn't quite trust her and wasn't about to set himself up again.

That didn't mean he couldn't talk about his business. "Since my ranch will specialize in bucking bulls, I had to search around for the right Brahmin sperm."

"I thought…don't all bulls buck?"

"Not necessarily. Breeders can actually produce

bulls that are prone to buck without using any of the cruelty devices I told you about."

"Wow. That's two new things I learned from you in the space of five minutes."

"Aren't you glad I came along tonight?"

She flashed a smile. "I certainly am."

The easy silence that fell between them didn't last long before Sarah slipped into anxious mode, her expression tense and her hands clasped tightly in her lap.

"Worried about tonight?" he asked.

"A little. I'm still not entirely comfortable around the Beckers. I found out that one of Mrs. Yancy's quilting friends used to know the family. Apparently they were super religious and very strict. Tammy had a rebellious streak, and they kept an iron grip on her and did everything they could to lead her down the 'right' path."

"And look how that turned out." Clay scoffed. "My parents didn't exactly go easy on me, but they were fair. Before I even had my first date, my dad pulled me aside and told me how to be safe." For which he silently thanked his father on a daily basis. "He didn't want me accidentally getting some girl pregnant."

"Ellen and I never had that talk, but she trusted me— as she should have. I was a student council member and an honors student, an all-around good girl."

Clay could see that. "So you weren't out having sex at sixteen." His first time had been exactly at that age.

"Not until my senior year, and we used birth control."

"Smart."

"No smarter than you and your girlfriends. Neither of us wanted me to get pregnant."

"Was it serious between you and him?"

"I thought so at the time, but we were heading for colleges in different states, and decided to break up.

Well, I did. I didn't want to start my freshman year involved with a guy who was seven hundred miles away. He's married now and has three children. What about you? Did you have a serious girlfriend in high school?"

"Yeah. We went steady for about a year." At the time Clay had thought he loved her, but after a while, realized he didn't. "She's been married and divorced twice and has a kid."

Sarah looked wistful. "I'd like to get married and have kids some day. And then stay married."

Clay imagined her with a couple of blue-eyed, black-haired kids. He didn't let himself think about her married. The thought of her with another man bothered him.

"I like kids," he said. "But I don't think I'll ever get married, so I won't be having any."

Sarah nodded, but didn't comment. For the rest of the drive, she didn't say another word. Clay chalked up her silence to nerves over the evening ahead.

He hoped the meal went well.

As SARAH AND CLAY followed her grandparents into the dining room, she was aware of the curious stares. It was obvious that people recognized Clay. Or maybe they just liked watching a gorgeous man saunter confidently across the room. Because Clay was exactly that—gorgeous and self-assured. He was especially striking in a sport coat and slacks, but he was also appealing in jeans and a T-shirt. Sarah suspected he'd look good in rags.

He'd said he never wanted to get married, but Sarah guessed that someday he would. After all, most guys, even those who had women hanging all over them, eventually settled down with one woman. At least for a while. He wasn't ready yet, that was all.

He touched the small of her back as they made their way toward the linen-clad table reserved for them, a possessive and intimate touch that filled her with warmth. Just for tonight, they belonged to each other.

Clay sat beside her at the table, with her grandparents across from them. The waiter brought menus and recited the specials before leaving them to make their decisions. They discussed the various cuts of meat, which Mr. Becker seemed an expert on. It turned out that he'd once been a butcher. A few minutes later, he gestured their server back.

After the waiter took their orders and left, Mr. Becker turned to Clay. "How was the drive over?"

"Easy, but traffic is always pretty light around here."

"Believe it or not, it used to be even lighter. The area seems to be growing. I sure don't know why."

They discussed the subject for a few moments before the conversation stalled.

"I spoke with Pete Charles and shared the information you gave me yesterday about Tammy," Sarah said in an effort to kill the awkward silence. "He promised to get back to me in a day or two. I'll let you know when I hear something."

A terse nod from Mr. Becker and nothing at all from his wife put an end to that topic. Apparently that subject was closed for the evening.

After a few more interminable seconds, Clay tried his hand at steering the conversation. "Your former house has a huge heated garage that I really appreciate."

Mr. Becker's eyes lit up. "I used to tinker with cars in there—a hobby of mine for years."

"I figured it was something like that," Clay said. "I keep my gym equipment there."

Mrs. Becker smiled. "You look like you're in good shape."

Sarah wasn't going to argue with that. He was in great shape.

"How did you two meet?" she asked.

"Sarah hasn't told you?"

Sarah shook her head and waited for Clay to explain, but he nodded at her to tell the story. "A few years go, I did an article on bull riding, featuring Clay," she summarized.

Expecting him to throw in a deprecating remark about that, she tensed. Instead, he surprised her by asking how she chose her topics.

"I try to balance what interests me with what I think the readers of the magazines I work for want to know," she said.

Her grandparents nodded, but neither replied. Apparently they were as bad at small talk as they were at expressing their feelings.

Dreading the clumsy silences, Sarah struggled throughout the meal to come up with things to talk about. Used to making chitchat with virtual strangers due to his rodeo fame, Clay smoothly picked up the slack.

Even with his easy sociability, carrying the conversation during the long dinner that was more an ordeal than a social get-together, took real skill. Sarah was impressed and intrigued. There were so many things she didn't know about Clay, qualities hidden beneath the surface. He never bragged about his talents, just quietly went about doing what was needed. She liked him all the more for that—far more than was wise.

Several times during the meal, he touched her in some way—gently bumping her with his arm or pressing his thigh to hers. Contact that only heightened her awareness of him.

From his hooded glances, she understood that he wasn't immune to those touches, either. His smoldering looks added to her anticipation. Surely everyone in the room felt the heat simmering between them.

Of all places to get hot and bothered—there, in the Sunset Manor dining room, seated with her newly found grandparents. To Sarah's relief they didn't seem to notice.

Determined to get hold of herself, she scooted her chair away from Clay. After that, there was no more physical contact or direct eye contact with him—neither of which helped at all. Despite not so much as glancing at him, she was aware of his every move. Feelings continued to simmer inside her—desire and need, and something far more dangerous.

The logical part of her mind warned her to stay safe and keep her distance, but her heart and body refused to listen.

By the time the waiter finally cleared away the dessert plates, she felt as if she were burning up from the inside out and was more than ready to leave.

To her relief, her grandparents didn't invite her and Clay up. They all headed for the lobby.

"Thanks for including me tonight," Clay said as he and Sarah waited with the Beckers for their elevator.

"Anytime." Mrs. Becker smiled and touched her hair. "Come back again."

Sarah could tell by her expression that she'd fallen under his spell—just like everyone who met him.

Clay shook hands with her grandfather and nodded at her grandmother before turning to Sarah. "Ready to go?"

"I am." Briefly she considered hugging her grandparents or kissing them goodbye, but she wasn't comfortable about expressing that kind of affection with them. "Good night," she said as they stepped into their elevator.

Clay cupped her elbow and steered her toward the exit. "That went well," he murmured for her ears only. "And I didn't even have to wear the tie."

"Thanks to you. If you hadn't kept the conversation going, who knows how we'd have survived."

"You'd have come up with something. Can I ask you a question?" She nodded. "Why do you call them Mr. and Mrs. Becker?"

"Because they said to call them Bob and Judy or Mr. and Mrs. Becker, and the latter is more comfortable for me."

"They don't want to be called Grandma and Grandpa, or something along those lines?"

Sarah shook her head. "But I don't mind, because right now, it wouldn't feel right."

BY THE TIME Clay exited Sunset Manor with Sarah, the sun was sinking toward the horizon and the air had cooled. Long shadows streaked the grounds, and brilliant bands of pink tinted the sky.

She glanced up, her face lit with pleasure. "What a gorgeous sunset."

"Beautiful," he agreed, but his eyes were on her. Finding it all but impossible to keep from touching her, he grasped her hand.

She was cold. He helped her into her shrug, a little thing that couldn't possibly protect her from the chill.

He itched to pull her into a dim corner and warm her

up, but the grounds of Sunset Manor were no place for what he had in mind.

"Here, put this on." He took off his sport coat and slipped it around her shoulders.

The jacket all but swallowed her up. She looked cute. He liked seeing her in something of his.

"Your grandmother reminds me of my mom's grandma—uptight and a little cold," he said as he started the pickup.

"My grandfather isn't much better. I'm used to that kind of behavior, though—Ellen was never very relaxed or affectionate. My dad was the opposite. After he died, the laughter and hugs were few and far between."

Clay had always taken his family's warmth for granted. He shook his head. "You said he died when you were ten."

"That's right. He was an engineer and an avid rock climber. He died in a freak accident on a mountain. My mother and I were out all afternoon. Back then, we didn't have cell phones, and the medics couldn't reach us. We found out when a reporter shared the story on the local news."

Clay couldn't even imagine. "That must've been a terrible shock."

"It was pretty awful." After a beat of silence, she said, "I missed him so much. I'm sure Ellen did, too, but she was stoic and insisted that I be strong, too. She didn't like it when I cried."

The thought of warm, expressive Sarah being told not to cry made Clay's chest ache. He didn't think much of her mother.

She fiddled with the strap of her purse. "It would've helped if I'd had brothers or sisters or aunts or uncles or some other family to grieve with, but it was just Ellen and me. I know I've already said this, but you're really lucky to have family."

"Now you do, too," he reminded her. "I saw the way your grandparents looked at you. They care. Maybe they're cautious, waiting for you to show them affection first."

"I wish it could just be natural." She sighed. "I just hope Pete finds Tammy. I really want to meet her, and ask her for the name of my biological father. I wonder if he and Tammy stayed in touch over the years."

"With any luck, you'll soon find out."

Sarah held up her crossed fingers. A blink later, her hopeful expression changed to something more bleak.

"You're looking pretty somber," Clay said.

"Tammy has stayed away from her parents since I was born, and as far as I know, she hasn't come looking for me. Why would she want to see me now?"

"Because you're her kid. Trust me, she'll want to know you." He reached for her hand again, and squeezed gently.

Sarah held on tight, as if soaking up his reassurance, before letting go.

They drove along in silence—a silence far different than any of the tense pauses during dinner. Sitting at the table beside Sarah tonight had kept Clay in a constant state of arousal. Hell, just thinking about her did that.

He was in trouble here, afraid he was getting in too deep. The smartest thing would be to drop her off at Mrs. Yancy's, head for his garage and work his leg until he was too sore and tired to think about sex. Like that had ever worked.

"It's early yet—too early to call it a night," he said.

"I know, but there isn't much to do around here in the evening."

"Oh, I can think of a few things. Let's go to my place. I'll open a couple of beers and show you my house plans."

He hadn't intended to bring up the blueprints, but now that he had, he wanted her to see what his house would look like. Since she wouldn't be here to see the finished product.

"Don't you mean etchings?" Her mouth twitched.

"I'm fresh out of those."

"Guess I'll have to settle for the house plans, then."

Hunger and promise darkened her eyes, and suddenly Clay wasn't thinking about house plans.

Chapter Fourteen

Sarah entered Clay's house with both longing and trepidation. Did she really want to do this?

In the kitchen, he popped open two beers and handed her one. "This is the only room in the house with an overhead light so it's the best place to look at the blueprints," he said, gesturing for her to sit at the table. "Hang tight while I grab them."

He might be playing it cool now, all focused on house plans, but they both knew what was going to happen later.

As the seconds ticked by, Sarah tried once again to reason with herself. Now was the perfect time to say she'd changed her mind and wanted to go back to Mrs. Yancy's.

The thing was, she wanted to stay. As long as she protected her heart, she'd be okay.

Clay returned to the room with the plans, and the heart she was supposed to keep safe sighed.

"You look awfully serious," he said. "What's on your mind?"

"Nothing, really." She managed a nod and a smile. "Let's see those plans."

Clay unrolled and spread the blueprints over the kitchen table. Standing behind her, he bent down and pointed out various details. He'd rolled up his shirt cuffs, and Sarah couldn't help noticing the sun-bronzed hair on his thick forearms and the clean, blunt nails on his hands. Hands that knew how to give pleasure.

Her mouth went dry. Hyperaware of his every move, she breathed in his clean scent and felt the heat from his body.

Or was all that warmth coming out of her?

"—wanted a circular floor plan, with big rooms and high ceilings," he was saying.

She forced herself to focus. "Very nice."

Which probably wasn't the "ooh, wow" his wonderful house deserved, but at the moment it was the best she could manage.

Leaning in close, he pointed to the second floor. "All the bedrooms will be up here," he said, his lips dangerously close to her ear. "The master suite will look out over the property."

She all but melted against him. He pointed out the fireplace, bath and adjoining office that made up his suite and then wrapped his arms around her from behind.

Heat pooled low in her belly. "It's…it's beautiful."

"You're beautiful," he growled, nipping her earlobe.

"Clay?" she managed, angling her head.

"Yeah?"

"Kiss me."

He pulled her to her feet and turned her so that she faced him. "Oh, I intend to," he said with such smoky sweetness that her whole body tingled. "I'm going to kiss you all over, until you're begging for more. Then I'm going to make love to you. That is, if you're ready."

She put her hands on his chest. "I've been ready for days now."

With a pleased sound, he pulled her into a searing kiss that took her breath away.

When he broke the kiss, they were both panting like runners after a race.

"Let's go to bed," he said, grabbing her hand and tugging her forward.

She wasn't sure her legs would support her, but somehow they did.

"I want you to know that it's been a while for me and that I'm clean," he said as he hurried her down the hall.

"Same here."

The drapes in his bedroom were already drawn, but dusky light crept through the crack where the drapes met. He quickly removed the bedspread.

The sheets looked fresh and clean. Dimly, she wondered whether he'd changed them because all along he'd known that she'd end up in his bed. Like every female he pursued.

Was she about to be one more in a countless string of women?

His deep, urgent kiss drowned out the doubts and every other thought in her head.

Then he was unzipping her dress and helping her out of it. He stared at her hungrily, and she was glad she'd worn her lavender satin-lace bra and matching bikini panties.

"You have the sexiest underwear." Without taking his gaze from hers, he shouldered out of his shirt and tossed it aside.

He was as perfect as she'd imagined, with broad, smooth shoulders, a smattering of hair on his chest and lean, hard abs.

Her attention drifted lower, to the arousal straining his fly. She unbuckled his belt, noting his hot, slitted gaze.

When she reached for the pull tab of his zipper, he sucked in a breath and held very still.

She worked the tab down, Clay groaning as her knuckles brushed his hard length.

In no time he stepped out of his pants and kicked them aside. He was wearing gray boxers that barely contained his erection. He was very well-endowed.

Then she saw the long red scar above his knee. "Is that from your recent accident?" she asked.

He nodded. "The one that ruined my career."

"Does it hurt?"

"Not at the moment." He pulled her into another kiss.

Then they were both naked, lying on the bed, sharing kisses and caresses that left her aching and drunk with feeling.

"You are the most beautiful woman," Clay whispered as he explored her body.

Every touch heightened her need, until she was desperate for more. When she was frantic, he knelt between her legs, parted her folds and licked the most sensitive part of her.

A low moan filled the air. Her own, she dimly realized. As she rocked her hips, he slid his fingers inside. His mouth still on her, he moved his fingers until she spiraled into a dazzling climax.

When at last she shuddered to a finish and lay still, he raised his head and grinned.

"You look awfully pleased with yourself," she said.

His gratified expression only deepened. "You seem pretty happy, too."

"I am. Now it's your turn." She smiled sweetly. "On your back, mister."

She kissed Clay's mouth, his chin, his neck. Licked his flat nipples and made her way down his torso, over muscled flesh and scars from old bull-riding injuries. When she reached his navel and started south, he sucked in his belly, slid his hands under her hair and cupped the back of her head, guiding her where he wanted her.

"Sweet Jesus," he murmured as she touched the velvety tip of his penis with her tongue.

She'd barely started exploring before he stopped her. Suddenly she was on her back with Clay over her. He kissed her hungrily and she caught fire all over again. "I want you inside me, Clay."

His eyes darkened. "Hold that thought."

He turned away and yanked open the drawer of the bedside table, sheathed himself, then positioned himself over her. "Now, where were we?"

"Here." Sarah arched up so that his arousal pressed against the place she most wanted him.

In one slick move, he slid into her, filling and stretching her. She gasped in pleasure.

Misinterpreting, Clay froze. "Too much, too fast?"

"Just right."

He pulled back so that he was hardly inside her, making her whimper. "Please, Clay."

With a growl he pushed in again, so deep, he became a part of her. "Better?"

There were no words to describe her feelings. "Oh, God, yes. Please don't stop."

He began the ancient, driving rhythm. The tension inside her tightened to the breaking point, and the whole world honed down to the place where they were joined.

A powerful climax began, and she forgot everything but Clay and the pleasure crashing through her.

UTTERLY DRAINED, CLAY fell against the pillow, keeping Sarah close. His leg hurt, but making love with her was more than worth any pain. He'd known women more skilled at sex, but no one had ever satisfied him like this.

He felt amazing. Whole.

Darkness had fallen, and the room was pitch-black. Wanting to see her, he flipped on the bedside table lamp.

Sarah blinked in the sudden light. She looked soft and thoroughly loved. *His*. He kissed her gently, then more deeply. Already he wanted her again, and knew that as soon his body recovered, he would make love with her a second time.

"That was awesome," he said.

"I'll say."

She ran her finger along his jaw and smiled into his eyes. She had little silver flecks in her blue irises, and she seemed to see straight into him. Not sure he liked that, he leaned in to kiss her again, stopping when his leg protested. The muscles were beginning to scream, telling him it was past time to pop two aspirin. "Stay put. I'll be right back with a washcloth," he said, hiding a wince as he pushed to his feet.

He downed the tablets, drinking water straight from the bathroom tap. Straightening, he rubbed the knotted muscles above his knee.

While he waited for the water to warm, he pulled a clean washcloth from the linen closet. He caught a glimpse of his reflection in the bathroom mirror and noted the sappy grin on his face. The same smile he'd seen on some of his buddies' faces from time to time, usually during the honeymoon part of a relationship.

Clay figured he finally understood that grin, and why he felt so happy—great sex. Make that fantastic sex, the best, ever. There was nothing like it.

ALONE IN CLAY'S big comfy bed, Sarah stretched and smiled. He was a wonderful lover—tender, thoughtful, caring and passionate all at once, and her whole body purred with satisfaction.

He was a great guy, period. He seemed to like her, too. She saw it in his eyes and his smile, and felt it in his pleasuring touch.

The words of the buckle bunny she'd overheard that afternoon three years ago popped into her mind. *The best I've ever had.*

Maybe he treated all his lovers in the same caring way. Regardless, Sarah knew he cared. Otherwise he wouldn't have searched the attic for the footlocker, or come with her to meet the Beckers that first time and again tonight.

He'd never made any promises, but she hadn't expected any. She was in no way ready to think about the future, and was pretty sure Clay wasn't, either. He hadn't even brought up the fact that she was leaving in less than a week, but neither had she.

For the time being, now was enough.

He padded in from the bathroom, naked, unselfconscious and gloriously masculine.

Instead of handing over the washcloth, he joined her in bed, the wicked glint in his eyes exciting and intoxicating.

"What are you going to do with that washcloth?" she asked.

"I always clean up after myself." He shot her a cocky grin and then burrowed under the covers.

How could a man with a washcloth turn her into a whimpering mess? A few heated moments later, he tossed the washcloth aside and made love to her again.

Later, glowing from the inside out, she snuggled

close and let out a contented sigh. The loudest growl she'd ever heard rumbled from Clay's belly.

"That sounds ominous," she teased.

His mouth quirked. "I've been working hard, and I need sustenance. How about you?"

It had only been a few hours since dinner, but Sarah hadn't eaten much. "I could eat," she said. "What've you got?"

"I'm thinking bacon and eggs. Wanna help me cook?"

"So that's why I'm here."

"That, and because I can't keep my hands off you." He traced her nipple with his finger. Desire licked through her. "Before you ravish me again, we need to feed you," she said. "Give me something to wear."

"Yes, ma'am." Clay tossed her his shirt. He grabbed a pair of jeans from a dresser drawer and pulled them on commando.

Some twenty minutes later, wearing panties and his shirt with the sleeves rolled up, Sarah sat down with him in the breakfast nook.

Without any preliminaries, Clay attacked his eggs. "This sure tastes good."

Surprised at how hungry she was, Sarah nodded around a mouthful.

When Clay finally came up for air, he studied her, his eyes dropping to half-mast. "You look sexy in my shirt."

The fabric smelled of him and brushed against her sensitive nipples, making them harden. She eyed his muscular chest. "You look sexy without it."

Heat flared in his eyes, and she wanted him all over again.

She wanted more than that, she realized while he mopped up egg yolk with his toast. A lot more.

Sometime tonight, she'd fallen in love with him. No, that wasn't quite true. If she were totally honest, she'd have to say that she'd started falling for him three years ago.

Admitting the truth to herself terrified her. Unable to take another bite, she set her fork down and pushed her half-eaten food aside.

Clay eyed the plate. "Are you going to finish that?"

"It's all yours."

He attacked her plate with gusto, never realizing that he owned her heart—hook, line and sinker.

There wasn't a thing she could do about it except enjoy what they shared for the few days she had left in town, then leave and pull herself together.

Chapter Fifteen

Clay was finishing the last of Sarah's eggs when his cell buzzed. Who'd call after eleven on a Friday night?

Back when he was at the top of his rodeo game, he'd fielded phone calls at all times of the night without missing a beat. But now? His life was low-key. No one called much past nine.

Unless there was an emergency of some kind at the ranch. "I'd better pick that up," he said. "It could be Mattson."

Sarah nodded. Her hair was tousled from their last go-around, and he could see the points of her nipples against his shirt. God help him, he wanted inside her again, as soon as possible.

He'd handle the call quickly, and then enjoy a steamy shower with her. His gaze on her, he lifted his hip and slid the phone from his back pocket and answered without checking the screen. "Clay here."

"Hey, Clay, this is Angela."

Unable to recognize the loud, slightly harsh voice, and not sure he knew anyone by that name, he frowned. "Who?"

"Angela Allen? We met in a bar in Billings some months ago?"

Now he remembered—the blonde with the big

breasts, the one he'd gotten plastered with. The last women he'd had sex with before Sarah.

He'd never expected or wanted to hear from her, and didn't welcome the call. Plus his number was unlisted. "How did you get my number?" he asked, none too friendly.

"It wasn't that difficult."

If that was true, he needed to change it. Wanting to get rid of her and get back to Sarah, he shrugged and rolled his eyes. He'd heard this before, and hoped to hell that, like Jeanne, Angela was lying. "What did you say you wanted?"

"There's something I need to tell you, and I really think we should talk about it in person. Can you meet me at the same bar tomorrow night?"

Having no desire to see her ever again, he frowned. "I don't live in Billings anymore. Whatever you have to say, say it now."

"Over the phone? But it's important."

"Just say it." He drummed his fingers impatiently on the table top.

"All right, if that's the way you want it. I'm pregnant."

"Okay. Congratulations, and have a great life."

"You don't understand. It's yours."

Caught off-guard, Clay was momentarily stunned. Not again. He didn't hide his scoff. "I don't think so. I may have drunk too much that night, but I remember using protection."

"The condom must've broken."

"If it had, we'd have known."

"Then there was a hole in it or something."

Bull.

"Clay!" she said so loudly he winced. "Are you there?"

"Oh, I'm here. Give me one good reason why I should believe you."

"Because I'm eighteen weeks along, which is about the time we slept together."

Clay quickly counted back. She was right, and despite his skepticism, doubts crept in. What if she was telling the truth?

"What are you going to do about it?" he asked warily.

"If you're asking whether I've considered an abortion, the answer is no. I want this baby."

He scrubbed his hand over his face. "What do you need from me?"

"As the father, you have certain responsibilities."

"You mean money."

"That's right. For medical bills and child support."

She was trying to trick him into paying for someone else's kid. It was either that, or he was going to be a father. Clay swore. "I want a DNA test."

"Fine, but I can't do that until after the baby is born."

Jeanne had been tested after her tenth week of pregnancy. "I happen to know that you can have one right now. Ask your doctor."

After a slight hesitation, she said, "I will."

"Good. I'll check with mine and get back to you."

"I'd appreciate that. Here's my phone number."

THE WOMAN ON the phone had a loud voice, and Sarah overheard almost everything she said. Her name was Angela, and she'd met Clay in a bar. She was pregnant and said he was responsible, just like the other woman he'd told her about.

He hadn't even recognized her name, a pretty good

indicator that the sex had probably been a quick, one-time thing. Which only reinforced the differences between Sarah and him. She had sex only with men she had real feelings for. But Clay took his sex lightly, as something to engage in with any willing woman.

She'd known this all along, and that was what made her so mad at herself. Getting involved with Clay, letting her feelings grow and deepen, was just plain foolish.

She watched him jot down Angela's number and suddenly wanted to get as far away from him as possible.

Looking somber, Clay hung up. "As Yogi Berra would say, that felt like déjà vu all over again. The woman on the phone claims to be carrying my baby, but I think she's lying. I always, always use protection."

"So you keep telling me, but as Angela said, the condom might have broken or been defective."

Clay raised his eyebrows. "You heard that?"

"Along with everything else she said."

"Wonderful," he muttered. "Look, what happened that night was before I decided to move to Saddlers Prairie and buy a ranch. I wasn't supposed to ever walk again, and was just out of a wheelchair, proving the doctors wrong.

"You'd think I'd have been happy about that, but I was feeling pretty sorry for myself. My career had tanked, and people I considered friends bailed on me. That was partly my fault, because after the accident I turned into a total ass. I was one pathetic piece of work—couldn't even stand my own company."

Scowling into the distance, he absently rubbed his knee. "One night, I drove to a tavern outside town, where I wouldn't run into anyone I knew. I wanted to get drunk fast, and I sat down at the bar and started drinking double scotches. At some point, Angela sat down next to me and struck up a conversation. That's how it happened. I hardly even remember what she looked like."

What could Sarah say to that? She simply listened.

"FYI, I haven't been with anyone since—until you," Clay added.

He gave her a level look, and she knew he was telling the truth. "And now Angela's pregnant," she said. "What are you going to do?"

"Same thing I did last time—get a paternity test and prove her wrong."

"And if *you* turn out to be wrong?"

The very suggestion skewed his solemn expression into a frown. "I'll cross that bridge if and when I have to." He scrubbed his face with both hands. "Look, it's getting late, and I need time to think."

Sarah understood. Under the same circumstances, she'd be shocked, too. She rose and carried her plate to the sink. "I'll get dressed."

Five minutes later, still reeling from Angela's call, Sarah climbed into Clay's pickup.

Neither of them spoke on the way to Mrs. Yancy's. Clay drove with his jaw set and his hands gripping the wheel, as tense as she'd ever seen him. No wonder that bull had thrown him.

Sarah wasn't exactly calm and relaxed, either. "Don't forget to breathe," she reminded him, attempting to lighten his mood.

He inhaled halfheartedly and exhaled, but the tension remained. Moments later, he parked in front of the house. At nearly midnight, only the porch light and a lamp in the living room greeted her. The rest of the house was dark. Mrs. Yancy must be asleep.

That suited Sarah fine. Before she faced her temporary landlady, she needed to pull herself together.

"I'm real sorry about this, Sarah." Leaving the engine running, Clay opened his door.

"Don't get out," she said.

"I want to walk you to the door."

"It's less than fifty feet away, and I'm a big girl. I can get there just fine by myself."

"I'll walk you, anyway." His eyes narrowed slightly, and she knew better than to argue with him.

They moved silently across the grass.

Between the ranch, the construction on his house and the business with Angela, Sarah doubted they'd see each other again before she left town. Which was probably for the best, but also meant that unless Clay planned to stay in touch, these were their last few moments together.

Standing under the porch light, she forced herself to meet his somber gaze. There was no glimmer of the warmth that had made her blood sing less than an hour earlier. True, he'd had a huge shock, but she knew he wasn't in love with her.

He liked her and enjoyed the sex, but he would never care for her as deeply as she wanted him to. She'd always known that, but had turned a blind eye.

Her heart felt as if it had cracked. Pressure built behind her eyes, signaling a headache and a big cry later. Somehow, she managed a bland expression. "Good luck with the test, Clay, and take care."

"Thanks. You, too."

Despite herself, she expected a light kiss, the gentle caress of his fingers on her cheek. Something.

But Clay only huffed out a heavy breath and kicked the toe of his boot at the porch floor. "I'll be in touch."

Right now he might think so, but Sarah doubted she'd hear from him again. He had a busy life that didn't include her.

Heavyhearted, she slipped through the front door.

Soft light bathed the living room in a welcoming glow that seemed to mock her pain. She waited until she heard the pickup drive off before flipping off the porch light and the lamp. Making her way through the blackness, she tiptoed up the stairs.

A hot shower washed Clay's scent from her skin, but did nothing to ease the icy chill inside her.

She'd lost him without ever having a chance at a relationship. Without ever having him at all.

Love sucked.

She stood under the spray and waited for the tears. But it was too soon, and the tears refused to come.

Exhausted by all that had happened, Sarah toweled herself off and pulled her nightie over her head. Craving the oblivion of sleep, she crawled into bed—a bed half the size of Clay's and twice as empty. Yet as dead tired as she was, she lay awake for a long time, replaying the unforgettable evening, ruined by one phone call.

A sobering wake-up call Sarah could've done without. She only wished it had come earlier.

A woman Clay barely knew might be carrying his baby. Before hooking up with her, he'd been in a wheelchair and not expected to walk again. He'd driven his friends away.

Until an hour ago, Sarah hadn't been aware of any of that.

She really didn't know him at all.

SARAH SLEPT IN Saturday morning, only waking when her chirping cell phone blasted her awake. It was after nine, late for her. But then, she'd fallen asleep just about the time the birds had started their predawn chatter.

Groggy and half thinking Clay might be calling, she reached for the phone before she remembered—he wasn't going to call.

The screen identified the caller as Pete Charles. Yawning, she pressed the talk button. "Good morning, Pete."

"Morning. I didn't wake you, did I?"

"Yes, but that's okay. What's up?"

"I'm afraid I have some bad news."

The words dissipated any vestiges of sleepiness. Sarah sat up. "Let me guess—you were unable to find Tammy."

"I'm afraid it's worse than that."

Okay, now she was both confused and worried. "What could possibly be worse?"

"Before I answer that question, I'd like to tell you what I uncovered. About twenty-eight years ago, Tammy settled in a Montana town called Big Timber, which is about two-hundred-and-sixty miles southwest of where you are now. Five years later, she married a man named Art Simmons. Her legal name was Tammy Simmons."

"Was? Did she divorce and change her name?"

"I wish that were the case. This is where I give you the bad news, so brace yourself."

Heart pounding, Sarah gripped the phone. "Go ahead."

Pete cleared his throat. "Unfortunately, Tammy passed away two years ago, at the age of forty-four. She was killed in a car accident. I'm really sorry, Sarah."

"Oh, dear God." Closing her eyes, Sarah sank against the headboard. The investigator remained silent, giving her time to absorb the information. "Did she and her husband have children?" she asked after a moment, wondering about half brothers or sisters.

"None. I do know that Tammy and Art owned a local sporting goods shop and fishing business, and that Art was quite a bit older. Not long after Tammy died, he sold the business. Within a year of his wife's death, he suffered a serious heart attack and passed away. Again, I'm sorry. I'll email you the link to the obituary."

"Thank you."

Numb and grief-stricken, Sarah disconnected. None of her questions would ever be answered.

She would never get to meet her biological mother, never learn the name of her biological father. Never know if Tammy had missed and thought about her over the years, and never find out why she'd stayed away from her parents.

Sarah hugged her pillow and thought about her grandparents. It was up to her to break this sad news to them. They would be devastated over losing their only child and filled with regret that they hadn't tried harder to find her.

If only she could call Clay. She needed him to hold and comfort her, and say things that would make her feel better. But he had problems of his own, and she doubted he wanted to hear any more about hers. Besides, she needed to start getting over him.

The tears that had refused to come last night finally fell. Sarah cried both for losing Tammy without ever having a chance to meet her and for losing Clay. Though she'd never really had him.

She was alone, but strong, and would deal with her grandparents and whatever else came her way just as she'd dealt with everything this past year. By herself.

Sarah squared her shoulders and got up.

Mrs. Yancy was probably waiting with breakfast for her. She would eat first. Then she would phone her grandparents and invite herself over so that she could break the news in person. Dreading the ordeal ahead, she made the bed, then padded into the bathroom.

After showering and dressing, she headed downstairs. The mouthwatering aroma she'd come to expect in the morning filled the air and stirred the appetite she thought she'd lost. Determined to hold herself together, she headed into the kitchen with her chin up.

"Good morning, Sarah." The older woman's eyes gleamed with curiosity. "You slept quite late. Clay must have kept you out until all hours."

At the mention of Clay, Sarah's composure slipped. She turned away to get coffee, but not quickly enough.

"Did you two have a fight last night?" Mrs. Yancy asked, sounding concerned.

"Nothing like that." Sarah brought her mug to the table and sank onto a chair.

"Then why do you look as if someone has died?"

The woman's sympathetic expression destroyed what was left of Sarah's tenuous grip on herself. "Someone did die—Tammy Becker," she said, her eyes filling. "The private investigator just called. She was killed in a car accident."

"Oh, honey." Mrs. Yancy left her post at the stove, brought Sarah a box of tissues and patted her shoulder. "I'm so sorry."

"Thank you." Sarah wiped her eyes.

"Does Clay know?"

Sarah shook her head. "He's—" Not about to air his dirty laundry, she hesitated. "He's dealing with some problems, and I don't think we'll be seeing each other again."

Her temporary landlady squeezed her shoulder, but thankfully didn't pry. "I'm serving pancakes this morning, which I happen to consider among the best comfort foods in the world—especially when loaded with chocolate chips. Are you ready for breakfast?"

"Yes, please."

"You sit tight and sip your coffee."

Mrs. Yancy had already eaten, but made herself a chocolaty pancake and joined Sarah at the table. Instead of breaking into her usual nonstop chatter, she left Sarah to her thoughts.

Grateful, Sarah sampled a pancake. It was delicious, and just what she needed. Ravenous for some reason, she devoured every crumb.

"Feel better now?" Mrs. Yancy asked.

"I actually do. I loved the chocolate chips. I've never had them in pancakes."

"Aren't they a nice addition? Tell me, do your grandparents know about Tammy?"

"Not yet. I'm going to call them in a little while and then drive over and see them."

"That's a good idea. I'll pack up some cookies to take along."

Sarah managed a smile. "That'd be nice."

"It's no trouble. Your grandparents are lucky you found them. You'll be a great comfort."

Sarah hoped so. Given the awkwardness between them and the lack of affection, she still wasn't sure they wanted to be grandparents.

"Clay seems so interested in your family, and very interested in you," Mrs. Yancy went on. "I'm sure that no matter how bad his problems are, he'll want you to share this with him."

Under normal circumstances she would, but Clay had other things on his mind. Besides, as bruised as Sarah's heart was, she didn't feel up to calling him. She ducked her head.

"You really like him."

Was it that obvious? She sighed. "I do."

"He feels the same about you. I can tell by the way he looks at you."

"I know that he likes me," she acceded, "but my feelings for him run deeper."

"Ah—you're in love with him. That was fast, but love sometimes works that way. It was like that with my John and me."

"I don't want to love Clay," Sarah said.

"You can't tell your heart who it should or shouldn't love."

Sarah sighed and nodded. "You're lucky you and your husband felt the same way about each other."

"Yes, and I've always been thankful for that. Clay may need more time, but you're perfect for him. He'll come around—I just know it. Whatever you do, don't give up."

There was nothing to give up. Clay already owned her heart. He was the best lover she'd ever known, but for him, sex was as casual as eating out. For Sarah, it meant so much more.

And that was probably the tip of the iceberg of differences between them, differences too wide to bridge.

"I could talk some sense into him," Mrs. Yancy added, straightening her spine.

Sarah cringed at the very thought. "Please don't."

"Whatever you say, dear. But I really think you could use his strong shoulder about now."

Because that was painfully true, Sarah made a quick decision. "I interviewed seven ranchers, met my grandparents and found out what happened to Tammy," she said. "I finished everything that I set out to do here, so there's no reason for me to stay through Wednesday. But don't worry, I'll pay for the full two weeks we agreed on."

She'd write the article at home and then work on the house until it was ready to put on the market. After that…Sarah wasn't sure where she'd live and didn't want to think about that now.

"I'm not sure whether I'll leave Monday or Tuesday," she went on. "That depends on how my grandparents handle Tammy's death."

Mrs. Yancy nodded. "I'll be sorry to see you go."

"You've been wonderful, but it's time for me to get back to Boise."

The woman looked unconvinced, and Sarah forced a smile. "I'll be okay. I always am."

Chapter Sixteen

Early Saturday morning Clay woke up with his mind in turmoil. He was pretty sure that he wasn't responsible for Angela's pregnancy, but doubted he'd be able to relax until they got the test results.

He'd been down this road before, but not in Saddlers Prairie, and had no idea where to go for the test. He'd ask Dr. Mark Engel, who ran the Saddlers Prairie Medical Clinic and was the only doctor in town.

Clay shoved both bed pillows under his head and caught a whiff of Sarah's perfume. Last night had been spectacular—at least until Angela's call.

If not for that, he had no doubt that Sarah would be here with him now. He imagined her asleep beside him, soft and naked and infinitely desirable. He'd kiss her awake. They'd fool around and end up making love—the best way in the world to start the day.

His hungry body was definitely on board, a certain part of him alert and ready. "Settle down," he said gruffly, and sat up.

As much as he wanted to be with her—and he wanted that more than just about anything—he wasn't stupid. That call had affected her, too, the shock on her face just about matching his own. Like him, she probably needed space to digest the whole sorry situation.

After putting himself through his usual killer work-out, he called the clinic and left a message for Dr. Mark's answering service. Then he headed for the ranch.

Several hours later, while Clay was busy helping the crew impregnate the cows and heifers, the good doctor returned his call. Clay snickered at the irony of his timing.

"I have to take this," he told Mattson.

"No problem."

Clay stepped out of eavesdropping range, wincing as his leg protested. "I can trust you to keep this to your-self, Doc, right?" he asked.

"Everything we discuss is confidential," Dr. Mark assured him.

Speaking in a low voice, Clay explained his situa-tion, adding that he didn't believe he was the father, and that although he always used protection, this wasn't the first time he'd needed a paternity test. "Where do I go to get the test around here and in Billings?" he asked.

"Let me look up a couple of labs in or near both cit-ies. I'll text you the addresses and phone numbers."

Less than five minutes later, armed with the info, Clay phoned Angela. He gave her a list of labs in Bill-ings. "As soon as you let me know where you're hav-ing your DNA test, I'll go to a local lab for my blood sample, and have them send it over," he said.

She didn't sound happy about that, which recon-firmed Clay's suspicions that he wasn't responsible for the pregnancy, and added that she needed to consult with her own doctor first. Her doctor didn't work week-ends, but Angela would call on Monday.

She continued to insist that Clay was the father. He didn't argue, just let her talk. Which turned out to be a smart move, as she finally ran out of steam. She agreed to get the test next week and let him know where to send his sample.

"Thank you," he said, relieved that she wasn't fighting him on this. "About a week after the lab receives both our tests, we'll know whether I'm the father."

When Clay disconnected, he felt better. Sometime in the next one to two weeks, he would know. God willing, the results would be in his favor.

He thought about updating Sarah, but decided to put off the call until he had something concrete to tell her. He'd call after Angela confirmed that she was going in for testing.

Then he and Sarah needed to talk. Clay wanted to make sure she understood what they'd already discussed—that he wasn't into serious. He wanted to keep seeing her for as long as his feelings lasted, but he couldn't commit to anything more than that.

He was pretty sure she wouldn't mind staying in touch. Too bad she lived as far away as Boise. Then again, Boise was on his list of cities to visit when his business was up and running. He would see Sarah there.

Which meant that, as of right now, Boise had just moved to the top of his list. In a much better mood, he rejoined his crew.

DREADING THE CALL she was about to make, Sarah dialed her grandparents from her bedroom.

"Hello, Sarah," Mr. Becker said. "If you're calling to thank us again for dinner, no need. We enjoyed seeing you and Clay. He doesn't act all full of himself like some celebrities. He's an interesting fella."

Her grandfather didn't know the half of it. "We had a good time, and I can't thank you enough. But I'm calling for a different reason. I heard from Pete Charles this morning."

"Oh?" Her grandfather sounded excited, which made what she was about to say that much more difficult. "Hold on, while I get my wife." He put his hand over the receiver, and Sarah heard his muffled voice. "Judy, pick up the phone. It's Sarah, and she heard from the private investigator."

A moment later, her grandmother spoke. "Hi, Sarah. Did your Mr. Charles find Tammy?"

"Yes, but I'm afraid it's bad news." Not sure how to tell them, she paused.

"Please, Sarah, tell us."

"Okay, but you might want to sit down." She pulled in a breath. "Two years ago, Tammy was in a car accident. She…" Her voice broke. "She didn't make it."

Her grandparents greeted this with silence. Then Mrs. Becker let out an odd wailing sound that stabbed right through Sarah's heart.

"My baby, gone?"

Mr. Becker cleared his throat and then swallowed thickly. "Tammy is with the Lord now."

Neither of them said another word. Sarah heard the quiet sobs. Grieving for them and for herself, she let her own tears flow freely down her cheeks.

After a moment, she reached for the tissues in her purse and dabbed her eyes. "I'm coming over."

Less than an hour later, she let herself into her grandparents' apartment.

Neither managed more than a nod of welcome.

Looking as if they'd been struck by lightning, they sat side by side on the sofa, just as they had the other day. Within range of touching each other but separate, grieving parents drawing a modicum of solace simply from each other's presence.

They might not be physically affectionate, but they loved and relied on each other. Sarah envied that, envied the bond they shared.

When her grandfather pulled himself together enough to notice the plate in her hands, she set it down. "Mrs. Yancy, the woman I'm staying with, sent these cookies and her condolences."

"Please thank her." Her grandmother struggled to her feet. "Coffee will go nicely with those. I started a fresh pot just before you called."

"Let me get it," Sarah said.

The older woman opened her mouth as if to argue, gave a weak nod and dropped back to the sofa. "All right."

After Sarah handed out the cups, she took a seat in the same armchair as before. No one touched the cookies or the coffee. The Beckers began to talk about Tammy.

"We were strict with her," Mr. Becker said almost apologetically. "But we did what we thought was best."

"She wouldn't tell us the name of the baby's father, even when we took away all her privileges," his wife said. "I read in her journal that it was someone who was with her on the youth group trip to Canada. A boy whose name started with the letter B. All those kids came from good, church-going families. I can't imagine who could've done that to our baby, and I have no idea whose name started with that letter."

"We attended the same church," Mr. Becker reminded her. "That didn't stop Tammy or the boy from doing what they did. Most of those families moved away long ago. I doubt we'll ever know his name."

"Whoever the boy was, he never let on, not even when Tammy disappeared. The minister and every member of our church tried to help, but even with prayer and their support, accepting that she was gone from our lives was a struggle." She began to cry quietly again. "We drove her away."

"You couldn't know she'd run off." A box of tissues sat on the coffee table. Sarah handed it to her grandmother. "You only did what you thought was best," she added, repeating her grandfather's earlier words.

Words that also applied to Ellen, Sarah realized. She'd kept the adoption a secret because, for whatever reasons, she'd thought it was the right thing to do.

Sarah had never considered Ellen's wants or needs, had only focused on the painful effects of her lie. She would never know why her adoptive mother had buried the truth, but seeing her in this new light blunted some of the anger and decreased the awful heaviness that had weighed her down since the day she'd found her birth certificate.

"She begged us to let her keep you, but we wouldn't even think about that," Mr. Becker said brokenly.

"We were too ashamed." Mrs. Becker hung her head. "Because of our stubborn pridefulness, we missed so much—watching our daughter mature and grow up. Getting to know you from the beginning."

Her heartfelt tone and regretful expression made Sarah's chest ache. Her grandparents might reject a hug, but she needed to give it.

Sarah stood, moved to the sofa and squeezed in between them. First she embraced her teary grandmother in a silent, comforting hug. Then she turned to her grandfather with open arms. He squeezed her hard, his shoulders shaking as he silently wept.

When she let go, they all blew their noses.

Suddenly Sarah's stomach growled. She glanced at the clock. She hadn't eaten since breakfast, and it was already midafternoon. Time to let the Beckers grieve alone and find a sandwich someplace.

"I should go now," she said. "But I can come back tomorrow."

"We'll be in church all day," her grandmother said. "If you'd like to attend with us, you're welcome."

Sarah didn't think she was up for that, and besides, she needed to work on the article. "Thanks, but I think I'll pass."

Mr. Becker opened his mouth, but his wife gave him a warning look. "We won't force you to come. That's another reason why we—" she choked up "—lost Tammy. We don't want to lose you, too."

Sarah knew she would dearly miss her grandparents when she returned to Boise. Maybe she should move closer. Something to think about later.

"I'd like to see you again before I leave for Boise," she said. "How about Monday?"

"That sounds fine," her grandmother said. "But I don't want to sit around the apartment and grieve. I need to keep busy."

"Is there something you'd like to do, Sarah?" her grandfather asked.

"I've looked around a little, but I'd love to explore more of the area. How about showing me some of your favorite places? I'll drive."

The Beckers both looked relieved at the suggestion.

"That'd be fine," her grandfather said. "Along the way, we'll have lunch someplace. There isn't much to see around here, but I suppose we could show you Red Deer, where we lived after we left Saddlers Prairie. It's a good forty miles from here, and bigger than Saddlers Prairie, but not as nice."

Sarah remembered the name of the town from when Clay had gone to the auction there. "Sure. I'd like to see it."

"All right. Clay's fairly new to this part of Montana. I wonder if he's been up there. Tell him he's welcome to join us."

Sarah bit her lip. "That's very nice of you. He was there recently for an auction, and right now he's pretty busy with his ranch."

"That's right, he bought that herd of cattle."

"Did you tell him about Tammy?" her grandmother asked, looking as if the answer mattered very much to her.

Sarah shook her head. "After I called you, I came straight here." Which, while true, wasn't the whole truth.

"I'm sure he'll want to know."

She sounded just like Mrs. Yancy. Not wanting to explain, Sarah busied herself clearing off the coffee table and loading the dishwasher.

"I'll see you Monday," she told the Beckers at the door.

"Sarah, will you do something for us?" her grandmother asked.

"Anything."

"Would you mind calling us Grandma and Grandpa?"

Her heart full, Sarah smiled. "I'd love to."

SATURDAY AND SUNDAY, between inseminating the cattle, tracking down a couple of heifers that had strayed off and dealing with a worrisome wolf sighting, Clay spent a busy weekend at the ranch. He hated leaving at the end of the day and looked forward to the time when his own house was finished and he could move in.

Late Monday morning, Angela phoned with the name of the lab her doctor had suggested for her blood test. She said she was going there the following day. Clay drove immediately to the Flagg Clinic lab in Elk Ridge, where he gave a blood sample and left instructions where to send it. The fifty-mile round trip was well worth the time and gas.

On the drive back to Saddlers Prairie, he thought about calling Sarah. He hadn't seen her since Friday night, and it felt like weeks. He would talk to her tonight. He reached the rental house with an empty belly and a burning desire to head for the ranch and lose himself in physical labor.

Shortly after he inhaled several PB and J sandwiches, someone knocked at his door. *Sarah.*

His heart hammered in his chest. He'd tell her now.

But instead of Sarah, Mrs. Yancy stood on the porch. "Hello, Clay," she said. "I'm glad I caught you at home. I brought you some cookies."

Not sure what she was up to, he studied her warily before accepting the plate. "Uh, thanks. Do you want to come in?"

"I'm due at a friend's soon, but I will for a minute or two."

He gestured her into the living room. She sat down on the sagging sofa that was probably older than Clay.

"I hope you don't mind my dropping by, but since I don't have your phone number, I—"

"Has something happened to Sarah?" he asked, suddenly tense and alert.

Mrs. Yancy's eyes widened. "She's all right."

Exhaling, he nodded, leaned against the wall and crossed his arms. "Then why are you here?"

"I like a man who gets right to the point. My John was the same way. By your reaction, I see that you two haven't talked this weekend."

"I've been busy with my ranch."

She nodded. "Sarah explained that you two won't be seeing each other again, but I thought she'd at least call you."

News to Clay, bad news if it was true. He definitely wanted to see more of Sarah, and had assumed she was of the same mind. Before he could think about it further, his visitor dropped her bomb.

"You probably aren't aware that she's decided to leave tomorrow morning instead of Wednesday."

Three years ago she'd behaved the same way, had cut out a day early without so much as a goodbye. Talk about the past smacking a guy in the face. "This is the first I've heard about that," Clay said.

Mrs. Yancy gave her head a sad shake. "I really hoped she would call and tell you what's happened."

Clay eyed her. "You said she was okay."

"In one sense, she is. Overall, though, she really isn't."

The woman talked in riddles. He cocked his eyebrow. "I don't have a clue what you're talking about. In plain English, tell me what's going on."

"All right, but she doesn't know that I'm here, and I'd appreciate it if you didn't say anything. I struggled all day yesterday and today over whether or not I should come when she asked me to stay out of this. But I think you should know that yesterday morning, she found out that Tammy died in a car accident a few years ago."

Clay wasn't sure what he'd expected to hear, but not

this. He'd bet his ranch that Sarah had never remotely considered that her biological mother had passed on.

She'd been so eager to find Tammy and get her questions answered. Now any chance of that was gone, and he could only guess at the pain she must be feeling.

He couldn't believe she hadn't called and told him, felt both sorry for her loss and furious that she'd kept something so important from him.

Didn't she get how much he cared?

Mrs. Yancy blinked in surprise, and he realized he was scowling. He quickly assumed the friendly expression he used with his fans. "Where is she now?" he asked mildly.

The woman exhaled. "She's spending the day with her grandparents. As you can imagine, they're pretty upset about Tammy, and she wanted to be with them before she left for Boise. I'll tell you, I'm going to miss that girl. She's been wonderful company."

She gave Clay a meaningful look, as if expecting him to comment that yeah, Sarah was the best, even if she did have a bad habit of taking off without a word. But she didn't pause long enough for him to open his mouth.

"Sarah picked them up at ten this morning, and they're showing her around the area. She said something about lunch in Red Deer."

A town Clay had visited twice. The other day, for the auction, and before that, to check out available ranchland. He hadn't been impressed. Size- and population-wise, the town was bigger than Saddlers Prairie, but not nearly as nice, and it was almost twice as far from Sunset Manor.

"Why would they take her to Red Deer?" he wondered.

"Sarah didn't say."

"Any idea when she'll be back?"

"She said she'd be back before dinner, but I don't know exactly when. She needs to pack tonight and whatnot, so I expect she'll be at the house in the next hour or so. When you talk to her, remind her that this is my potluck and quilting bee night, and that I won't be back until after eleven."

Mrs. Yancy looked him right in the eye, practically ordering him to make good use of the privacy.

Clay intended to do just that. He and Sarah needed to straighten out a few things. For starters, that he wasn't about to let her waltz out of his life again. He definitely wanted to keep seeing her. He also wanted to be there for her, especially now, when she needed him.

In the grand scheme of his life, he wasn't sure what that meant. He only knew that he wasn't letting her skip out without seeing her and talking face-to-face.

After letting Mattson know he wouldn't make it to the ranch that day, he climbed into the pickup and headed for Mrs. Yancy's to wait for Sarah.

Chapter Seventeen

By the time Sarah tearfully hugged her grandparents goodbye and dropped them off Monday afternoon, she'd spent over six hours in the car. Smart move, doing all that exploring the day before the long drive back to Boise.

As she headed up the highway toward Saddlers Prairie, she thought about the grief and joy that had filled her day—sorrow over losing Tammy before ever having the chance to meet her and happiness at connecting with her grandparents.

She'd promised to come back again soon, and was leaning strongly toward moving closer to them. She certainly liked the area—except for Red Deer. It was too far away from Sunset Manor and seemed tired and drab, and not at all welcoming.

Sarah preferred Saddlers Prairie. The rolling plains and the huge expanse of sky overhead felt right to her, as though she'd come home. Her roots were here, so in a sense, she had.

But she wasn't ready to make such a big decision just yet and hadn't mentioned the idea.

If she were to move, living in the same town as Clay could be awkward, especially when she was in love with him. On the other hand, they were both adults. Surely they could handle the occasional meeting.

Anyway, she had plenty of time to make up her mind, since fixing up the house in Boise and getting it sold was bound to take a while.

Mrs. Yancy's street was just ahead. Sarah glanced at the digital clock on the dash. It was after five. No doubt, her busy landlady had already left for her quilting party.

Sarah envied her robust social life. Her own evening loomed ahead like a dull penny. Dinner and packing for the drive home would take up some of her time. But then what?

As she turned onto the street, a wave of loneliness flooded her. Quickly she pushed it aside. No pity parties allowed. She'd find a movie on TV tonight, and make buttered popcorn. Any movie would… Sarah squinted at what looked like Clay's pickup parked out front. Afraid she might be hallucinating, she blinked a few times.

No, that *was* his pickup.

He was sprawled on the stoop, leaning back on his elbows, his long legs crossed at the ankles and a piece of hay clasped firmly between his lips. The perfect picture of a gorgeous man on a lazy afternoon.

Sarah's wayward heart lifted. Frowning, she parked behind the truck. What in the world was he doing here?

Clay tossed the hay and straightened, and she knew she was about to find out.

As SERIOUSLY PISSED off as Clay was, he blanked his expression and pushed to his feet with none of the anger he felt.

"You're leaving tomorrow morning," he said by way of greeting. "You're supposed to stay until Wednesday."

She raised her chin defensively. "Hello to you, too. It's only one day early. I accomplished everything I set out to do when I arrived in Saddlers Prairie, and there really isn't anything left for me here. Who told you, anyway?"

Nothing left for her here? That stung. "Like you, I never divulge my source." Clay gestured at the stoop. "Sit down."

"I can't. I have to pack."

"You'll have plenty of time later. Sit," he ordered, using the tone that meant business.

"Oh, all right." She sat down, perching stiffly on the concrete edge.

Clay joined her. "I heard about Tammy," he said. "I'm sorry."

"It's so sad." She bent down and plucked a dandelion bud by the stem. "Mrs. Yancy told you a lot," she said, muttering something about her landlady's big mouth.

"I'm glad someone did."

She looked at him sideways, and he shook his head. "I've been in on this search for her since the day you showed up at my place," he said. "I found the foot-locker, called you to come get it and was there when you opened it. I drove you to meet your grandparents for the first time, and I sat through a pretty uncomfortable dinner with them. I figure I've earned the right to hear about something that important."

She had her eyes on that dandelion bud, so he cupped her chin and forced eyed contact. "Dammit, Sarah, why didn't you tell me?"

"Because right now you have so much on your plate."

"We all do. You still could've—*should*'ve—told me."

"Okay. I'm sorry!"

She jerked her head away, but not before he saw the

remorse on her face. Somewhat mollified, he blew out a breath. "Apology accepted. How are you dealing with Tammy's death?"

Her shoulders slumped. "It hurts. I hate that I'll never meet her, and never find out who my father is."

"At least you know what happened to her."

"There is that."

"How are your grandparents doing?"

"As you can imagine, they're devastated. They're also dealing with guilt and regret. They wish they'd been more accepting of the pregnancy and wish they'd searched harder for her."

As Sarah talked, she began to relax, and the tense knot in Clay's belly loosened. "That's got to be hard on them," he said. "And on you."

"It's been rough, but something good has come out of the pain. They asked me to call them Grandma and Grandpa."

Joy shone from her eyes, making her so beautiful that Clay almost forgot to breathe. Feelings he didn't want to examine flooded his chest, and he could no longer hold on to his anger.

He wanted to wrap Sarah in his arms and hold her close, but right now, things between them were pretty tenuous. "That's great," he said, leaning back on his hands. "Now they really are your family."

"Yes." She smiled. "This is going to sound strange, but I also realized something about Ellen. She kept the truth from me because, for whatever reason, she thought it was the right thing to do. I'll never know why, but at least I understand that she had the best intentions."

"Interesting insight."

"And very freeing."

"So I see," he said. "You look a hundred years lighter."

"Really? Wow, that's pretty cool."

Her expression was as open now as before Angela's call the other night. The feelings in Clay's chest spilled over and filled his body and soul with warmth and tenderness.

What was that about? Not ready to explore the question, he changed the subject. "I had the blood test done today, and had it sent to the lab running Angela's part of the test. In five to ten business days I'll know."

Sarah nodded and fiddled with the dandelion.

"I've done some thinking about the baby," he went on. "If I am the father, and I'm pretty sure I'm not, I want to be a part of his or her life. I don't want my kid to go through what you're going through, forever wondering about the man who fathered you."

"For the baby's sake, I think that's great," she said.

"That doesn't mean I want anything to do with Angela. I never did. That night was a mistake."

Sarah's expression shuttered closed.

Was Angela the reason she'd pulled back?

"Spit it out, Sarah. What's on your mind?"

She shrugged. "You've always moved from woman to woman."

Guilty as charged. He raised a wary eyebrow.

"And that's okay. You don't have to worry about me, Clay. I'm fine."

She was giving him a pass for the other night, and he ought to count his blessings. He didn't. "So this is goodbye," he guessed.

"Well, I am leaving tomorrow. I don't know when I'll be back, and you're bound to meet other women. I'm just being realistic."

At the moment, Sarah was the only one he wanted.

Which wasn't all that surprising. The real kicker was that at some point during the past two weeks, he'd changed. He wanted Sarah in his future.

That scared him spitless, and he sat up straight. Before he said anything, he needed to think about it. Yet the words tumbled out anyway. "I'm not ready for goodbye."

SARAH KNEW BETTER than to trust Clay's words. He wanted to keep the door open and see her from time to time, but that wouldn't work for her. Three years ago she'd started to fall for him. Now he owned her heart, and spending occasional nights together wouldn't be enough. Besides, if she wanted to get over him and move on with her life, she needed to end things now.

She let out a heavy sigh. "We're two very different people, Clay."

"I don't see that as a problem. It keeps life interesting."

His penetrating gaze only deepened the crack in her heart. Afraid she might say something she'd regret, she tossed the dandelion aside. "Look, I have things to do. I really should go in."

She started to stand, but Clay cupped her shoulder, forcing her to remain seated. "You can't just walk away in the middle of a conversation."

He looked at her with the dark intensity that turned her bones to liquid. Steeling herself, she glanced at her sandals. "There really isn't anything to say."

His laugh was utterly devoid of humor. "You make love with me like you mean it and then suddenly decide you're not going to see me again, and there's nothing to say? Give me a break, Sarah."

"All right, since you asked." She ducked out of his grasp. "You and I are complete opposites, and yes, that might make life interesting, but we'd never work. Why put ourselves through that kind of hell?"

Dammit, she was going to tear up. She blinked hard.

Clay brushed her bangs aside, his rough, masculine fingers gentle and warm. "How are we opposites?" he asked in a soft voice.

"We don't want the same things. I see myself married someday. You prefer the single life. I want kids. You may end up with one, but only because of a drunken mistake."

"See, I think we have a lot in common. We like each other. We can talk about all kinds of stuff, even if we disagree, and enjoy the conversation. And the sex is dynamite," he added in a low, sexy voice while he ran the pad of his thumb over her bottom lip.

Delicious shivers eddied through her. Just when she was about to melt into a puddle of need, his eyes narrowed and he dropped his hand. "But the real issue here is that you're running away from me, just like you did before."

Sarah scoffed. "I don't run away from people. As I already explained, I finished my research early, both this time and before. It didn't make any sense for me to stick around then, and it doesn't now."

"So you snuck away without a word. Then you ignored every one of my calls, texts and emails. You were afraid of getting involved with me then, and you're just as afraid now."

That he saw through her so easily scared her a little. "You never wanted a relationship—just sex. I understand, and I thought I could handle that, but I was wrong."

He went very still, his expression impossible to read. "You're saying you want a relationship with me?"

Oh, crap, she should've kept that to herself. She stood up. "Please, let me go inside while I still have a shred of self-respect left."

Clay pushed to his feet, wincing. His leg probably hurt. He caught hold of her hand and cleared his throat.

"I have feelings for you, Sarah. Sexual feelings, but also something more." He swallowed as if nervous. "I'll be honest—I'm not sure where any of it will lead. But if you're game, I'd like to find out."

Words she'd never imagined hearing and wasn't sure she trusted. Clay, wanting to explore his feelings for her? Who knew where that might lead? Wary, she frowned. "But I'm leaving."

"True, but over the next few months I'll be traveling around, introducing myself and my new business to rodeo owners across the West. It just so happens that Boise is one of the cities on my list. In fact, I'll be there a lot. Let me see you when I'm in town."

He was asking her to take a huge risk, a risk that could end up hurting her even more than she hurt now. She bit her lip. "I need to think about it."

"You do that."

He kissed her lightly on the mouth. Just enough that her mind emptied and her body began to hum.

All too soon, he let her go. "I'll let you know about the paternity test. Travel safe, and expect a call from me soon."

Chapter Eighteen

Early Friday evening Clay grabbed a beer, propped his leg on a couple of pillows and called Sarah. His first call to her since she'd left town.

"Hello?" she asked, sounding distracted.

"It's Clay, checking to see if you made it home."

"Hi," she said, the warmth in her voice indicating that she was pleased to hear from him. "I made it without a hitch. I drove straight through, and got in late Tuesday night."

"Sounds like a long day."

"Thirteen-plus hours of driving. How are you?"

Where to begin? "It's been a rough few days," he said. "The rain started Tuesday night and didn't stop until a few hours ago. The river that cuts through the ranch overflowed, and my crew and I worked pretty much 24/7 to keep the damage to a minimum."

His leg hurt like hell. He was going to rest it tonight and part of tomorrow.

"That's awful. Are your cattle okay?"

"We lost two heifers, but the rest are fine."

"What a shame. I'll bet you're tired," she said.

"Dead on my feet. Right now, I'm sprawled out on the couch, sipping a beer."

Sarah asked about damage to the ranches she'd visited, and Clay filled her in. "Glad to be home?" he asked.

"To tell you the truth, the house is a little too quiet. I actually miss Mrs. Yancy's chatter."

They both laughed, and the conversation wound down. Time to cut to the chase. "Are you gonna let me see you when I come to Boise?"

"When will that be?"

"Not for a couple of weeks."

She was quiet for so long, he wondered if she'd walked away from the phone.

"I'm still thinking about it," she finally said.

That didn't sound good, but was better than a flat-out "no." Clay wished he could think of a way to convince her that he was serious about exploring the connection between them. Much to his own surprise, he was just as serious about that as the other night.

He decided to leave the subject alone for now. "No problem. How's the article coming?"

"Not so well. I've been struggling with it for hours. I have tons of great information, and I've written a rough draft, but it's pretty flat. It needs something, but I can't figure out what."

"Would an interview from Saddlers Prairie's one and only stock contractor help?"

He heard her breath of surprise. "But I thought… You said you didn't want to—"

"A man can change his mind."

"I guess so," she said, sounding skeptical. "What brought that about?"

"Before, I didn't trust you. Now, I do," he admitted, still amazed at that.

"Oh," she said softly, and he sensed that she was smiling. "Hang on while I grab my recorder and open a new document."

THANK YOU SO much, Clay," she said when she finished interviewing him a while later. "The article won't be out for a few months, but I'll send you a copy. And this time, I swear, I'll only say nice things about you."

"You'd better," Clay teased. If things went the way he wanted them to, she'd put that copy directly into his hands. "I'll call you again soon."

TAKING A BREAK from painting the walls, which was doing wonders for the formerly dingy kitchen, Sarah marveled at all she'd accomplished in the eight days since she'd returned to Boise. The day before yesterday she'd finished the ranching article and emailed it to her editor.

Almost immediately, an editor from a different magazine had asked for an article on small businesses that were succeeding in spite of the tough economic times. Sarah had started researching companies and finding contacts to interview.

She'd also talked with a realtor, purchased paint and painting supplies, rolled up her sleeves and set to work. Painting the whole interior would take several weeks.

If that wasn't enough, drawers and closets needed emptying, and the basement needed a thorough cleaning. The realtor had also suggested replacing some of the carpeting and a major overhaul on the yard. For that, Sarah had scheduled the carpet layers and hired a landscaping crew. The rest she intended to tackle by herself. If all went well, she'd put the house up for sale in early July, about a month from now.

Which gave her plenty of time to decide if she wanted to live in Saddlers Prairie. Clay called nearly every day, but for some reason Sarah couldn't explain, she hadn't mentioned that she planned to move or that she was fixing up the house to sell. She hadn't given him her answer yet, either. To her relief, he hadn't pressured her.

Ready to get back to work, she dipped the roller into a tray of paint. Her mind wandered to the past and various boyfriends from high school, college and beyond. Thinking back, she realized she'd always found reasons to break up before things progressed too far—a pattern that had continued right up through Matthew. Months before moving home to take care of Ellen she'd pushed him away, using Ellen's cancer as an excuse to end the relationship.

Sarah was mulling over her track record and rolling paint up the wall when a startling realization hit her.

Since her father's death, she'd been afraid that if she cared too much for a man, he would leave.

She stopped painting. Excess paint from the roller dribbled on her forearm. Absently wiping her arm on her paint-splattered jeans, she marveled at the illogical belief her ten-year-old brain had manufactured. Somehow, she'd never let go of that belief, hadn't even realized until now that she held it.

Which meant that Clay was right—she *had* been running away from him. From love.

He'd allowed her to interview him because he trusted her. Maybe it was time to set her fears aside and trust him—stay invested in their relationship and see what happened.

A relationship with Clay. At that heady thought, she laughed out loud. She definitely wanted to see him again.

Now that she'd made up her mind, she could hardly wait to tell him. She wished she could drive over to his house and talk to him in person, but a call would have to do. She set the roller aside and washed her hands. She was pulling her cell phone from her hip pocket when it rang. *Clay* showed on the screen.

Grinning, she picked up. "I was just about to call you."

"No kidding. You sound happy. What's up?"

"You first." It was too early for him to break for lunch. There was only one reason why he'd call now. "You got the test results." Squeezing her eyes shut, she crossed her fingers.

"Yep, and they came out exactly as I suspected— I'm not the father of the baby Angela is carrying. She was trying to get her hands on my money. Believe it or not, she apologized and said she was going to contact the real father."

Sarah let out a relieved breath. If Clay were here, she'd throw her arms around him. "I hope things works out for her and the baby. I don't understand people like that."

"Me, either. Your turn."

"I've been doing a lot of thinking about us and what you said the night before I left. You're right, Clay, I was running away. I don't want to do that anymore."

The simple act of telling him made her feel lighter and freer than she could ever remember.

Clay whooped, and she laughed and did a little shimmy.

"There's more to say, but first, when are you coming to Boise?" she asked.

"Well..." The doorbell chimes cut him off. "Better answer that."

"Whoever it is can wait."

The doorbell chimed again, and just kept chiming.

"If I were you, I'd answer that."

"I will, and believe me, I'm going to give whoever it is a piece of my mind. Hold on."

Cupping the phone and frowning, Sarah opened the door. Clay stood there, wearing a grin that crinkled his eyes. Her jaw dropped. "What are you doing here? I didn't expect to see you for at least another week."

"Gotta hang up now," he said, slipping his phone into his pocket.

She barely had time to stuff her own phone away before he pulled her close and kissed her.

When he let her go, Sarah felt breathless and dazed. "I got paint on your jeans," she managed.

"I have plenty more pairs at home. I'm here because I couldn't wait another week to see you. We need to talk. Let's go inside."

CLAY PUT HIS arm around Sarah, keeping her close. If all went well, he would never let her go. Sometime during the night he'd finally made sense of his strong feelings for her.

For the first time in his life, he was in love.

He loved Sarah.

Finally he understood what all the fuss was about. Yet, as good as he felt, she might not want his love. Baring his soul to her was risky, but a risk he needed to take.

"By my clothes, the mess in here and the paint fumes, you probably guessed that I'm fixing up the house," she said. "It's going to look so much better."

So she wanted to live here. Clay's heart sank. That put a big crimp in his plans. But they could work things out. "You got paint on your face, too," he pointed out, touching her forehead and the tip of her nose.

"Oh, great," she muttered. "Getting that off should be fun. Painting isn't exactly my favorite job, but the realtor says that if I want the best price for this place, I need to spruce it up."

"You're selling," he said, feeling a lot better.

She nodded. "This was Ellen's house. I'm ready to let it go and start fresh."

"Any idea where you'll live?" He sucked in a breath.

"That all depends. I'd like to be closer to my grandparents, but I don't want you to think I'm chasing after you." Her eyes twinkled.

He broke into a grin. "You don't have to chase me—I'm already yours."

"Am I hearing correctly? Mr. I Don't Do Serious has changed his—"

Clay shut her up with another kiss, this one longer and hotter than the one at the door. He wanted to pull her into the bedroom, but not until he said what he needed to say.

"Hey, come back here," she said when he broke contact.

"All in good time. We need to talk."

"That's right. I haven't finished telling you what I wanted to say." She swallowed nervously and locked her hands at her waist. "I made a decision about us."

Clay's heart stopped dead in his chest.

"I'm with you—I think we should definitely see where this relationship goes," she said.

It wasn't exactly a declaration of love, but it was a start. He blew out a breath and decided to go for broke. "We need to talk more about that. Is there someplace we can go where the fumes aren't so toxic?"

The light in her eyes faded into worry. "There's a patio table on the back porch."

Sarah led him to a screened porch at the back of the house. As he sat down across the table, she gave him a dirty look.

"Don't you dare tell me you changed your mind."

Clay chuckled. "That's one of the things I love about you—you're not afraid to say what you're thinking."

This was it, the moment of truth. He cleared his throat. "Now it's my turn. I never figured I'd fall in love. Then you walked into my life with your attitudes and opinions and your strength and intelligence. You turned my world upside down, and I love you for it. I love you, period, Sarah Tigarden."

She blinked, and a soft smile curved her lips. "You know something, Clay? We really are a lot alike. Because I love you, too. I think I have since I first met you three years ago."

Suddenly Clay was on top of the world. He felt better than he had after winning his first championship. His chest full to bursting, he stood and held out his hands. "Let me show you what I think of that."

He kissed her with all the love inside him.

Releasing the sweet sigh that was forever branded on his soul, she sank against him. And he was home. He wanted her so badly his knees threatened to buckle. "Where's the bedroom?" he asked.

Linking her fingers through his, she led him up the stairs. "I don't use Ellen's room, and I should warn you, my bed is pretty small."

"That'll work."

Later, when they were both sated and Sarah lay curled at his side, she lifted her head. "Will you help me find a place to live in Saddlers Prairie?"

"Yeah, but I don't think you should buy."

"Why not?"

Because if things worked out the way he hoped, she'd be moving in with him. He traced her beautiful face with his finger. "It's a good idea to keep your options open. You know, in case things work out between us and we end up married."

She smiled. "I like the way you think, cowboy."

Epilogue

Three years later

"Wake up, honey," Clay murmured, touching Sarah's shoulder. "Your grandparents and Mrs. Yancy are downstairs."

Groggy from a much-needed nap, Sarah lurched up. "But I haven't dressed the twins—"

"I managed that—with some help from my mom and sister. In fact, I dressed them each twice. You don't want to know what happened the first time. Let's just say, those clothes are now in the wash."

Sarah laughed and thanked her lucky stars for a husband as wonderful as Clay, and for his special family, who accepted her as one of their own. His whole extended family had arrived while she was in labor, and had been among the first to welcome Olivia Tamara and Jayden Clay Hollyer to the world.

A few days later, the men and Clay's aunt and nieces had returned to Billings, leaving his mom, sister and both grandmothers here for two awesome weeks. They'd been a great help, making Sarah's suddenly hectic and demanding life easier.

She stood. Frowning, she smoothed her sleep-wrinkled clothes. "I'd better change."

"You're fine." Clay tipped up her chin. "I love you very much." He kissed her softly.

As always, she melted against him. When she came up for air, she cupped his strong jaw, gazed into his warm eyes and smiled. "I love you, too, but we both know that I still have twenty-five pounds to lose."

"You look perfect to me. Remember what Dr. Mark said. Nursing will burn off any excess weight in no time—especially with the hearty appetites our babies have."

"Just like their daddy."

As exhausted as Sarah was, she wouldn't change a thing about her life. Clay, the babies, his thriving business, their gorgeous, custom-built home. The friends she'd made, living on the ranch. She had everything she'd ever dreamed of, and more.

And it had all started with Ellen's secret and the search for Tammy Becker. "Thank you, Ellen," she whispered.

"What was that?" Clay asked.

"I'm just so thankful for you and what we have together." Sarah took his hand. "Let's go downstairs."

* * * * *

COMING NEXT MONTH
from Harlequin® American Romance®

AVAILABLE JULY 1, 2013

#1457 BRANDED BY A CALLAHAN
Callahan Cowboys
Tina Leonard

Dante Callahan never dreamed that the nanny he's had his eye on has her eyes on him. But when Ana St. John seduces him, Dante's determined to make her his!

#1458 THE RANCHER'S HOMECOMING
Sweetheart, Nevada
Cathy McDavid

Sam Wyler returns to Sweetheart, a storybook place for eloping couples, to breathe new life into the town and win back Annie Hennessy—if she can only forgive him for his sins of long ago.

#1459 THE COWBOY NEXT DOOR
The Cash Brothers
Marin Thomas

Cowboy Johnny Cash has always thought of Shannon Douglas as a little sister. But when they bump into each other at a rodeo, the lady bull rider seems all grown-up...and just his type!

#1460 PROMISE FROM A COWBOY
Coffee Creek, Montana
C.J. Carmichael

When new evidence surfaces from an old crime, rodeo cowboy B. J. Lambert finally returns home. Not to defend himself, as Sheriff Savannah Moody thinks—but to protect *her*.

You can find more information on upcoming Harlequin® titles, free excerpts and more at www.Harlequin.com.

HARCNM0613

REQUEST YOUR FREE BOOKS!
2 FREE NOVELS PLUS 2 FREE GIFTS!

◆ HARLEQUIN®

American ★ Romance®

LOVE, HOME & HAPPINESS

YES! Please send me 2 FREE Harlequin® American Romance® novels and my 2 FREE gifts (gifts are worth about $10). After receiving them, if I don't wish to receive any more books, I can return the shipping statement marked "cancel." If I don't cancel, I will receive 4 brand-new novels every month and be billed just $4.74 per book in the U.S. or $5.24 per book in Canada. That's a savings of at least 14% off the cover price! It's quite a bargain! Shipping and handling is just 50¢ per book in the U.S. and 75¢ per book in Canada.* I understand that accepting the 2 free books and gifts places me under no obligation to buy anything. I can always return a shipment and cancel at any time. Even if I never buy another book, the two free books and gifts are mine to keep forever.

154/354 HDN F4YN

Name	(PLEASE PRINT)

Address	Apt. #

City	State/Prov.	Zip/Postal Code

Signature (if under 18, a parent or guardian must sign)

Mail to the Harlequin® Reader Service:
IN U.S.A.: P.O. Box 1867, Buffalo, NY 14240-1867
IN CANADA: P.O. Box 609, Fort Erie, Ontario L2A 5X3

Want to try two free books from another line?
Call 1-800-873-8635 or visit www.ReaderService.com.

* Terms and prices subject to change without notice. Prices do not include applicable taxes. Sales tax applicable in N.Y. Canadian residents will be charged applicable taxes. Offer not valid in Quebec. This offer is limited to one order per household. Not valid for current subscribers to Harlequin American Romance books. All orders subject to credit approval. Credit or debit balances in a customer's account(s) may be offset by any other outstanding balance owed by or to the customer. Please allow 4 to 6 weeks for delivery. Offer available while quantities last.

Your Privacy—The Harlequin® Reader Service is committed to protecting your privacy. Our Privacy Policy is available online at www.ReaderService.com or upon request from the Harlequin Reader Service.

We make a portion of our mailing list available to reputable third parties that offer products we believe may interest you. If you prefer that we not exchange your name with third parties, or if you wish to clarify or modify your communication preferences, please visit us at www.ReaderService.com/consumerschoice or write to us at Harlequin Reader Service Preference Service, P.O. Box 9062, Buffalo, NY 14269. Include your complete name and address.

HAR13R

SPECIAL EXCERPT FROM

HARLEQUIN®

American ★ Romance®

Looking for another great Western read?
Read on for a sneak peek of

THE RANCHER'S HOMECOMING

by Cathy McDavid

**July's Harlequin
Recommended Read!**

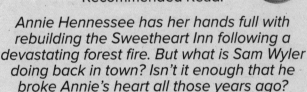

*Annie Hennessee has her hands full with
rebuilding the Sweetheart Inn following a
devastating forest fire. But what is Sam Wyler
doing back in town? Isn't it enough that he
broke Annie's heart all those years ago?*

A figure emerged from the shadows. A man. He wore jeans and
boots, and a black cowboy hat was pulled low over his brow.

Even so, she instantly recognized him, and her broken heart
beat as if it was brand-new.

Sam! He was back. After nine years.

Why? And what was he doing at the Gold Nugget?

"Annie?" He started down the stairs, the confused expression
on his face changing to one of recognition. "It's you!"

Suddenly nervous, she retreated. If he hadn't seen her, she'd
have run.

No, that was a stupid reaction. She wasn't young and vulnerable
anymore. She was thirty-four. The mother of a three-year-old
child. Grown. Confident. Strong.

And yet the door beckoned. He'd always had that effect on her,
been able to strip away her defenses.

A rush of irritation, more at herself than him, galvanized her.

"What are you doing here?"

Ignoring her question, he descended the stairs, his boots making contact with the wooden steps one at a time. Lord, it seemed to take forever.

This wasn't, she recalled, the first time he'd kept her waiting. Or the longest.

At last he stood before her, tall, handsome and every inch the rugged cowboy she remembered.

"Hey, girl, how are you? I wasn't sure you still lived in Sweetheart."

He spoke with an ease that gave no hint of those last angry words they'd exchanged, and he even used his once-familiar endearment for her. He might have swept her into a hug if Annie hadn't stepped to the side.

"Still here."

"I heard about the inn." Regret filled his voice. "I'm sorry."

"Me, too." She lifted her chin. "We're going to rebuild. As soon as we settle with the insurance company."

"You look good." His gaze never left her face. She was grateful he didn't seem to notice her khaki uniform, rumpled and soiled after a day in the field. Or her hair escaping her ponytail and hanging in limp tendrils. Her lack of makeup.

"Th-thank you."

"Been a while."

"Quite a while."

His blue eyes transfixed her, as they always had, and she felt her bones melt.

Dammit! Her entire world had fallen apart the past six weeks. She didn't need Sam showing up, kicking at the pieces.

Will Sam turn out to be a help or a hindrance to Annie's attempts to rebuild her life?

Find out in THE RANCHER'S HOMECOMING by Cathy McDavid, book one of her new SWEETHEART, NEVADA trilogy.

Available in July 2013, only from Harlequin American Romance.

SADDLE UP AND READ 'EM!

This summer, get your fix of Western reads and pick up a cowboy from the HOME & FAMILY category in July!

BRANDED BY A CALLAHAN by Tina Leonard,
Callahan Cowboys
Harlequin American Romance

THE RANCHER'S HOMECOMING by Cathy McDavid,
Sweetheart, Nevada
Harlequin American Romance

MAROONED WITH THE MAVERICK by Christine Rimmer,
Montana Mavericks
Harlequin Special Edition

CELEBRATION'S BRIDE by Nancy Robards Thompson,
Celebrations, Inc.
Harlequin Special Edition

*Look for these great Western reads AND MORE,
available wherever books are sold or visit*
www.Harlequin.com/Westerns

HARLEQUIN

American ★ Romance®

Another Callahan Cowboys story from
USA TODAY bestselling author

TINA LEONARD

Marriage isn't in Dante Callahan's short-term plans.
But Ana St. John is! After the gorgeous nanny
bodyguard—and woman of his fantasies—turns the
tables and seduces *him*, Dante is suddenly corralling
his inner wild man. Now Ana is having his baby…and
refusing to say "I do"!

He may be crazy for pulling out all stops to get Ana to
marry him—but that's part of the fun of being a Callahan!

Branded by a Callahan

**Available July 1
from Harlequin® American Romance®.**

Meet THE CASH BROTHERS, six sexy rodeo cowboys. It takes a special woman to lasso one of these men!

Hardworking cowboy Johnny Cash has always been a protector to his little sister's best friend, sweet but tough cowgirl Shannon Douglas. It's pretty crazy for girls to ride bulls—but absolutely no way can he fall for the boss's daughter....

Johnny's protectiveness drives her crazy...the same way his kisses do. Her heart says he's the one—but her own stubborn streak might push him away.

The Cowboy Next Door
by MARIN THOMAS

Book one in THE CASH BROTHERS series

**Available July 1
from Harlequin® American Romance®.**

HARLEQUIN®

American ★ Romance®

A Cowboy with Something to Hide…

On the rodeo circuit, B. J. Lambert had plenty of chances to forget about his first love. Back in Coffee Creek, it's impossible. Savannah Moody is as irresistible to B.J. as when they were teens. He'd still do anything for her—except give up the secret he promised to keep.

Sheriff Savannah Moody knows B.J. is hiding something. But she simply can't afford to give in to her attraction. She has family to care for and a job to do: to pursue the truth and discover what really happened eighteen years ago. Even if it costs her dearly…

Promise from a Cowboy

by C.J. CARMICHAEL

**Available July 1
from Harlequin® American Romance®.**